A random meeting on a train
going to Toronto.

A missing girl from Montreal.

A nightmare begins again.

Inspired by actual events.

Let Sleeping Dogs Lie

by

Pico Triano

PUBLISHED BY:
Inknbeans Press

Cover: Evonne

Let Sleeping Dogs Lie
© 2013 Pico Triano
and Inknbeans Press

ISBN-13: 978-0615823935 (Inknbeans Press)

ISBN-10: 0615823939

Chapter I

Someone always makes it aboard the train just before departure. The porter dragged an enormous suitcase through the door, and pushed it into the baggage area with a grunt and a hint of annoyance written on his face. Through it all, the late arrival peppered him with questions in French as he guided her toward her seat. Mark Rathman watched with amusement as the little drama moved down the aisle toward him, until he realized that the only empty spot in the entire train car sat right next to him. At least this chatterbox wasn't speaking English. He didn't ride the train to socialize. The train started moving before she reached her seat. She gave Mark a nervous smile as she sat.

"Voudriez-vous, changer de siege avec moi, et vous pouvez regardez dehors?" Mark asked in heavily accented, stilted French. Downtown Montreal, Quebec rolled by as the Via Rail train left the station. Mark couldn't help notice the view of Montreal from the rail lines, old brickwork, graffiti and bits of garbage.

"That's very nice of you to offer," the young woman responded in flawless English. "Are you sure you don't want to sit by the window yourself?"

"No, no..." Mark said, caught off guard, "I plan to sleep most of the way to Toronto anyway."

1

Her smile faded some in disappointment when he said he would sleep. He slid over to the aisle end of the bench seat while she squeezed past him. He caught a whiff of her hair as she passed much closer than he wanted.

"Thank you," she said, once she'd settled into her seat. "You're a gentleman."

Being nice wasn't his intention. He really wanted to catch some shuteye and avoid any unnecessary social contact. He wanted to blend in and disappear like a ghost. Before boarding he noted an off duty police officer travelling with his wife and two Canadian Armed Forces personnel on leave. Probably going home to visit family. If they were looking to party they were going the wrong direction. No threats to him, though. Goons from Rodrigues' gang were even less subtle in public. He could spot them a mile away. He wasn't particularly concerned about blowing his cover. His identification would pass close inspection and his enemies didn't have a clue where he'd disappeared off to anyway.

"By the way, my name is Christine."

Great, she wants to have a conversation. Worse, he couldn't help but notice her brown eyes, the shape of her small nose and mouth, her expression as she spoke. God, even with blond hair she looked way too much like Nicole. A painful hollowness filled his chest. He regretted taking the train, even if he could stretch out his long legs, and sleep in relative comfort.

"Nice to meet you. I'm Phil," Mark lied with a straight face. "Hope you don't mind my sleeping."

"It's okay, I'm pretty tired myself. I won't bother you."

To Mark's surprise she left him to sleep after that. The presence of an attractive woman in the seat next to him made falling asleep a challenge. His skin tingled. His mind kept drifting back to her image and he had to fight the urge to look again. He sensed her attraction and struggled to hide his own, unintentional interest. He could feel her looking at him out of the corner of her eye. A year and a half since Nicole's murder and the loneliness still ate into him as strong as ever. Finally, she stopped watching him and turned to look out the window as the last of Montreal slipped from view.

Spring began settling into the fertile St. Lawrence valley, and the landscape showed signs of exploding into green glory. As the train progressed, the blazing sun that shone when they departed, gave way to cloud, dark and brooding. Mark drifted off to sleep before they passed Cornwall, a fine drizzle pelted against the window. Christine herself nodded off a little later, tipping over and snuggling into Mark's side.

Mark's quiet trip proceeded to get further derailed. He drew attention to himself as he slept, haunted by a recurring nightmare that picked this place and time to torture him again. He awoke wild-eyed and tense somewhere past Kingston.

"Are you ok, Phil?" Christine asked, awakened by his thrashing.

Mark fought through a mental fog. She had invaded his dream as its final victim. His waking up had transformed her expression of terror to that of concerned stranger in a baffling instant. Other passengers stared. At least he knew that he told her his name was Phil. He used that name a lot.

"Just a bit of a nightmare is all," he stammered out. "Might've been something I ate before I got on the train."

"Should watch what you eat," she said relaxing just a little. "Must've been an awful nightmare. You were starting to make a scene with all that tossing, turning, muttering and yelling out like that."

The fog started to lift for Mark now, and things began to make sense. Christine's face bore that remarkable resemblance to Nicole, he'd noticed earlier, pretty but with an air of innocence that Nicole never had. If not for the blond hair, they could've passed for sisters. Her build and manner were similar to Nicole's as well, petite, with a girlish figure. He figured his subconscious grabbed a hold of that and prompted this version of his recurring nightmare. A dose of hormones probably worked against him, as well. She appeared to be blushing a little, which struck him a little odd. He cursed himself for taking public transportation. Dreams like this haunted him every once in a while. Part of him worried about losing his edge. Not being at the top of his game could prove deadly. Rodrigues and his organization would not allow him a mistake. If he were caught, he would die without seeing justice. He knew too much and had caused them too much grief.

"Is your wife coming to pick you up at the train station?"

The question caught him off guard. It took him a moment to realize, her eyes rested on the plain wedding band on his finger. Taking the train looked more and more like a terrible mistake. He should have just driven the van.

"No, I live by myself. My wife died in a car crash a little more than a year ago," he lied. "Icy roads, heavy traffic..."

"I am so sorry. I had no idea."

Mark shifted in his seat a little. The lies usually came so easily, and Christine just accepted it all, oblivious to his dishonesty. Something about her made him ashamed about lying to her, even if it was necessary.

Since he couldn't avoid a conversation, he thought it best to start giving it a little direction. Take it somewhere, way away from explaining his life. After all, it would be more than an hour before the train would arrive at Union Station in Toronto.

"What brings you to the big city?" he asked.

"I met recruiters who offered me a job and a small apartment." The words gushed out of her mouth. "I impressed them with my secretarial skills, and the fact that I have no accent in French or English. I've never traveled much, so I'm really excited."

"Good for you! Have you ever been to Toronto?"

"No," she said dropping her eyes to her hands folded in her lap. "I've barely been outside of the eastern townships. I've been to Montreal a few times. For us, the big city was Granby...believe it or not."

"Nothing wrong with being a small town girl, don't let the big city turn you into a cold-hearted business executive."

"It isn't that bad is it?" She looked back up at him her eyes widening.

"Naw, I'm just teasing a little." He answered, a hint of a smile teasing the corner of his mouth. "I loved the townships, and the people there. I just think you are going to find Toronto a little bit cold in comparison. Don't let me kill your enthusiasm though. There are lots of opportunities, and all kinds of different people. It took me awhile to get used to it."

"You are not from Toronto then?"

"I am for now," he replied. "Grew up in Niagara Falls, went to college in California, even lived in Montreal for awhile." He cursed himself because he didn't want to get the conversation back on himself or tell her much about himself. She seemed more concerned about learning the details of her new hometown, and the conversation centred on that the rest of the way to Toronto.

The train pulled into Union Station right on time, 5:30PM. They both needed to take the subway, so they agreed to stick together until Christine got to her stop.

When they stood in the aisle next to each other, Christine looked up at Mark, just a little wide-eyed.

"What?" Mark asked.

"I'm sorry, I just had no idea you were so tall. I feel like a midget. We look funny together."

Mark just gave her a little half smile for that one. "C'mon, let's grab our bags and get out of here."

They followed the inching line of passengers, down the aisle to the exit, where they picked up their luggage. Mark's suitcase appeared small next to Christine's awkward monster. She held up the line, trying to get it turned around, so she could grab the strap to pull it along behind her.

Mark looked back, and only hesitated a few seconds before grabbing the handle and hefting it easily. He didn't put it down until they were clear of the train, and out of the mass of people moving toward the subway.

"Wow, I sure could've used you going from the bus terminal to the train station back in Montreal," Her voice was tinged with a note of awe.

"You dragged this, all the way across Place Bonaventure? I'm impressed. How'd you manage all those stairs?"

"Some old man had pity on me, and with his help we managed. I almost missed the train because of that."

"This next bit is going to be a very, rude welcome to Toronto. It's rush hour, so here's what we'll do." Mark spoke, fumbling in his pocket. "I got an extra subway token here somewhere from before I got my pass."

He found the token and passed it to Christine. "I'm going to carry your suitcase backwards, and you're going to hold the strap, so we don't get separated. Ready?"

She nodded and they were off. The crowd closed around them. No need to worry about getting lost. Everyone rushed in the same direction. Mark was ready for it, and had the advantage of at least being able to see ahead. He felt sorry for Christine, knowing that all she could see were bodies crushing in around her. At the ticket booth, Mark already had his pass out, and waved it at the attendant in the booth. Christine dropped her token into the turn style and walked through. They stopped on the edge of the platform, a little way away from the bulk of the crowd.

"That was smooth." He grinned trying to encourage a very bewildered Christine. "Just relax for a second. The subway doors will stop right in front of us here. There's a breeze coming out of the tunnel. Should be able to hear it soon."

As predicted, the subway rolled to a stop, and they were standing right in front of the doors to the last car. They carried everything in and there were even seats available. They sat. Christine pulled a piece of paper and pen out of her purse, and jotted a couple things down as they pulled out of the station.

Mark gave her a gentle nudge, "You're getting off at College. It isn't very far. I'll help you out of the station with that oversized suitcase of yours, and you can catch a cab from there as you were planning. It shouldn't cost you too much. I have a pass and can get back on the subway, no problem. I'm not in a great hurry."

"I really appreciate all you've done to help me. I don't know how I would have managed to get this far without your help." she answered. Then she added, "And to think if I'd known you were a giant, I would have been scared of you and not said two words to you all the way here. You just don't seem so huge when you're sitting down."

He grinned at her. "Too friendly for my own good."

He could see the tension building in her facial features as they approached the point of parting ways. His mind flashed back to his nightmare, and her frightened image echoed in the back of his mind. He shrugged it off, knowing his subconscious struggled to make sense of things that didn't have to make any sense. Either that or his testosterone levels were getting out of hand. He looked into her eyes and he sensed the hollowness inside him again. Part of Mark missed that kind of companionship. He missed Nicole more than ever. He wanted to follow Christine like a lost puppy. No time for that, he had a destiny to fulfill, a war to fight. Christine, or anyone else, would just be a distraction and maybe another casualty.

The College subway station flashed into view. The doors opened and they were off to the races again. Hordes of people swarmed around them as they climbed the stairs on their way out to the street. When they breathed the not so fresh air of wet downtown Toronto, Christine looked bewildered. Mark knew exactly where they were going and where they needed to be. He hailed a cab for her and got her suitcase into the trunk. Time to part and Christine looked petrified. She pressed the piece of paper she had written on, into Mark's hand.

"This is the phone number and address of the company I will be working for. I'll let them know to take a message or transfer you through to me. Please call, I would love to see you again." She stated this almost pleadingly, and the images and words from his nightmare echoed in his mind again.

"Sure," he lied. He didn't intend to ever see her again, and the lie almost stuck in his throat. Maybe, if things were different, he could pursue a relationship, but not now. He shook it off. Don't kid yourself. He already had the love of his life, and he lost her. He blamed himself. He stuffed the note in his pocket after pretending to look at it. He smiled at her and felt like a hypocrite. Good thing this was ending now. He didn't want to hurt her feelings... or his for that matter.

He shut the door to the cab, and waved as it disappeared into the late afternoon Toronto traffic. Now he felt like crap. This would mess with his head for days. He picked up his suitcase resting on the ground, which suddenly seemed a whole lot heavier than before. There were new gadgets in there that he looked forward to putting to work. That would have to wait till tomorrow.

Right now he needed to get back on the subway and ride. Home waited at the end of the line in the back of his plain brown and gold Ford Econoline van. He looked forward to settling down on his cot, and catching up on the sleep he didn't get on the train. Next time he had to go to Montreal he would just drive there. His hand rested for a moment on the pocket where he had stuffed Christine's note. For a moment, he thought about pulling it out and having a look at it. The temptation toyed with him, but he decided he would go to sleep and make a point of forgetting. For some reason, he couldn't just crumple it and throw it in the nearest trashcan.

Chapter II

The cab door closed beside her with a dull thud. Christine's heart skipped a beat with the sound. Doubts came flooding into her mind.

"Where to, lady?" asked the turbaned cabbie.

"Um...six Wylie Street," she responded.

"Ah, Gabbagetown," he smiled. At least he looked harmless.

Christine watched Phil wave as they set off and then he disappeared into the bustle of downtown Toronto. She looked back for a moment hoping to catch a final glimpse of him, before pulling her gaze forward again. A thought struck her.

"Excuse me. Did you just say Garbagetown?"

"No, no Gabbagetown. Not far. Don't worry. Just lots of cars now."

She didn't push the issue. With the man's accent, it wasn't clear what he was saying. Her thoughts drifted back to Phil as Toronto crowded around the cab. How embarrassing to wake up leaning against him on the train. Such a contrast to Martin, her jerk ex-boyfriend. She then laughed at herself inside for a second. She just got to town fell in love and slept with the first man she met. She would have laughed out loud, but she didn't want the cab driver to think her crazy woman.

"You want I drive fast?"

Her knuckles whitened as she gripped the armrest. "No, please take your time. I'm not in a hurry." They were weaving through heavy rush hour traffic a great deal faster than she was comfortable with already. She let out a sigh of relief as the light ahead turned red and traffic ground to a halt.

The cabbie turned to her and flashed a toothy smile. "First visit to Toronto?"

She nodded yes, but turned away. His eyes were kind, but she wanted to be alone with her thoughts, while they inched toward the address for Toronto City Adventures.   He understood and let her be.

Stuck in downtown Toronto reminded her of Montreal. The buildings were newer though and the streets seemed to be wider. The train had passed through the rain but the skies were still overcast. The gloom got her mind thinking about the events of the last few days.

Martin the jackass, was the start of all this and likely knew she was gone by now. Provided he'd gotten over his latest hangover. Maybe he went drinking with his buddies again without even seeing the "I hope I never see you again note". They'd had a big fight. He had a few more beers and contented himself under the hood of that stupid car of his. She took off to Granby with her friend Sonja who wanted to go dancing. No, she wasn't in the mood for dancing or drinking or anything, just sat in a chair nursing a non-alcoholic fruit juice. Some Anglophone guy thought to hit on her, but she sent him packing. After that Bernard Fortin came and introduced himself.

"You don't look like you want to be here," were the first words out of his mouth.

She remembered looking daggers at him thinking he was trying to pick her up. He was on a different kind of mission though. He was in town for a few days hoping to recruit some talent for a company called Toronto City Adventures a tourism company based out of Toronto. He hadn't met with a whole lot of luck during his stay to that point. In fact, he'd given up on the day and dropped by for a drink. Couldn't help but notice her fluent rebuff of bozo number one. They discussed the opportunity at some length. He left her with the company website so she could check it out on her own time. He also gave her a phone number to call if she was interested and the name of a Brenda Cooper who might be available to interview her right over the phone. He asked for her name and nothing else and told her he would give the company an endorsement if she chose to follow up.

Martin got to sleep on the couch for the next few nights. While he was still comatose early in the morning, she'd gone online and researched this company, Toronto City Adventures. It looked like the real deal. She came away impressed and called Brenda as soon as she got home from work that evening. Bernard had given them quite a glowing report and the interview went well.

Toronto City Adventures invited her to come to Toronto and sent return bus and train tickets by express mail. She was advised to travel with the intention of starting immediately when she got there. Accommodations would be provided until she could find her own. She worried about asking for a week off her current job, but that turned out to be no problem at all. She felt there was nothing to lose and everything to gain. If all went well, she would escape a lousy employment situation, a lousy relationship and show her family she could take care of herself in one shot. She looked forward to flaunting her success to her mom.

The cab lurched forward again as traffic began to thin out. Train tracks in the middle of the road seemed odd until they passed a red and white Toronto transit trolley. Out of the city core they passed a couple of churches with green copper roofs that reminded her of pictures of the parliament building in Ottawa. The buildings got smaller and older. The trees along the road surprised her, and she imagined when the leaves were developed they would look nice.

Weaving through a few small streets they found Wylie Street at last. The six-story building they pulled up in front of wasn't anything to get excited about. She had pictured a sleek office building and this looked more like a drab apartment house. As the cabbie helped her get her baggage out of the trunk, she couldn't help but see the stairs leading to the front door. She felt a twinge of doubt.

"That's a heavy suitcase for such a lettle gurl," the cabbie commented as she counted out her fare. She didn't much like the statement even though he said it without malice.

He waited at the end of the walk, while she grabbed the strap of her suitcase and dragged it to the base of the steps. She ignored him and her doubts and started the epic struggle to get everything to the top of those cursed steps. The cab sped off as the door to the building opened. The receptionist had noticed her through the glass door and came to the rescue.

"You must be Christine," said a warm, resonant voice.

Christine smiled, "You then must be Brenda."

Brenda didn't look anything as she expected. Over the phone, she pictured a young, motherly figure. Reality showed a modern thirtyish woman flaunting a great deal of cleavage. The two of them working together managed to heave the suitcase to the landing at the top of the stone steps.

"You don't believe in travelling light do you?" Brenda gasped, catching her breath.

Christine responded with a shy smile and embarrassed shrug. Getting the rest of the way into the building wasn't as challenging. Brenda held the door while Christine dragged her luggage over the final half step into the lobby.

"I got bad news for you, honey," Brenda said, pulling a face. "Our elevator is out of order, and the room we prepared for you is all the way at the top. I had my work out for the day with you on the front steps and you look way too scrawny to manage to bring it up yourself. That means you're going to have to leave it down here for the time being. Zap runs this place, and he isn't going to be back till late tonight. I'll have him bring it up tomorrow when he comes up for your first business meeting."

Christine put on her best brave face. "I can grab a couple of things out of it before I go up and make do until then."

"Good. How was your trip then?"

"Long and tiring. Met a nice man on the train. Handled that suitcase of mine like it weighed nothing."

"Ooo... Always good to have some man muscle around. Did you get his number?"

Christine rolled her eyes. "No. He was real polite and helpful... I think he was just tolerating me though."

"I don't know about that. My experience with men tells that when a man is nice he wants more."

"He told me he lost his wife in a car accident and I don't think he's over it."

"That's sad. Too bad for you. Sounds like an alright guy."

Something occurred to Christine and she couldn't help but ask, "Why did the cab driver call this part of Toronto Garbagetown?"

Brenda looked puzzled for a moment and then burst out laughing. "It's called Cabbagetown and we're just on the edge of it. Your cabbie had a big accent didn't he?"

Christine laughed until she felt tears on her cheeks. "I'm sorry. It really sounded like Garbagetown to me."

Regaining her composure, Brenda yanked open one of the drawers on her desk, and rummaged around, until she found the set of keys for the room. She then handed them to Christine.

"I better get you on your way. Number 603; just climb those stairs over there all the way to the top. It's down the hall. You shouldn't be able to miss it. I'll come up and help you get settled later."

Before heading up, Christine quickly opened up the suitcase, grabbed some clean underwear, her pyjamas and a small bag with toiletries.

"Have you had anything to eat?" Brenda asked before Christine finished.

"Actually, now that you mention it; the last thing I ate was a snack on the train a few hours ago. Are there any nearby restaurants where I could grab something?"

"Nothing convenient but I could bring something up for you. Save you the trouble. Any particular likes or dislikes?"

"I'm really not that fussy."

"Burger and fries make you happy?"

"That'd be fine."

"Good. My treat. You get yourself upstairs and don't worry about a thing."

Christine looked around her as she made the ascent. The lobby appeared nice enough, but as she made her way up the stairs, the stairway and halls screamed cheap hotel rather than fine business establishment. It even seemed a bit creepy. On the other hand, it didn't smell dirty and dingy, and she didn't get the impression she would encounter a rat at the next turn, so maybe it wasn't so bad.

When she got to the top, she found 603 without any trouble. She pushed her key into the doorknob, turned it, held her breath, and pushed the door open. She let out a gasp of disbelief. Her "room" turned out to be a beautiful small apartment, four rooms, a small office, a generous bedroom with a double bed, a kitchenette with a cook top and fridge, and a beautiful bathroom with a heart shaped spa type bathtub. Better than she could have ever imagined. She didn't care for the overabundance of mirrors in the bathroom, though. A large, flat screen, high definition TV adorned the wall at the foot of the bed in the bedroom.

She found each room tastefully but conservatively decorated, which surprised her after seeing the rest of the building first. She felt like a little girl as she tested her gadgets. She bounced on the bed, but couldn't figure out how to turn on the TV. She even gave the electric can opener in the kitchen a dry run. The computer in the office wasn't hooked up yet. That didn't bother her too much. Zap would see to it that all the office machines were hooked up before she started working. Zap... She rolled the nickname around in her head. Sounded like some kind of thug rather than a businessman. She couldn't help a nagging doubt niggling in the back of her mind and focusing on her employer's nickname gave her a foreboding shudder.

After more than a half hour, Brenda made her appearance with supper. Christine ate with gusto.

"You like it?" Brenda asked, gesturing around her.

"It's beautiful," Christine answered. "I don't think it could be much better."

"Glad you like it," Brenda continued. "Later we may move you to a lower floor. Here you get to start at the top and work your way down. Have you figured out how all the gadgets work?"

"I tried some of the stuff but I don't know how the TV works."

"I can help you with that."

They marched into the bedroom where Brenda opened a drawer, pulled out a remote control and turned on the TV. "You're in for a treat. This button here lets you access the guide and from there you can watch anything you like. More channels than you can count. We subscribe to everything and I mean everything. If there's a channel you can't watch, something is either wrong with the signal or something's wrong with the TV."

The demonstration impressed Christine. They went back to the office and Brenda motioned for her to sit down. Christine sat behind her desk and Brenda pulled up a chair across from her.

"Tomorrow morning we get right down to business. Try to get lots of sleep tonight. At eight o'clock, I will be coming with Zap to have a breakfast meeting. We need to take blood tests and a urine sample. That may sound weird to you, but we deal with clientele from all over the world some of them quite wealthy. We have a zero tolerance drug policy. Have you ever used any recreational narcotics or other illegal substances?"

"I tried some pot once with some of my friends in high school but I haven't used it since."

"At least you're being honest with me," Brenda reassured her. "Something like that would never show on a test. Just relax. I'm sure you'll be fine. What do you want for breakfast?"

"Just some cereal would be fine. I'll probably be too nervous to eat too much."

"Okay we'll bring you up a selection when we come in the morning," replied Brenda. "After breakfast Zap will run through your orientation. I gotta get back down to the lobby now. See you tomorrow."

With that, Brenda up and left Christine to herself. Christine thought to go watch some TV but first she wanted to go soak in the bathtub. She rarely enjoyed that luxury; she was tired and a bit sore from traveling. She went into the bathroom found some bubble bath, and started to run a tub of water. While the bath filled, she went to the bedroom, took off her little business suit, and hung it up with care, so that it wouldn't get wrinkled. She preferred to wear something fresh in the morning for her meeting with the boss, but her suitcase still languished in the lobby. Besides, she wore this outfit to try and impress them as a secretary/business woman. She found slippers, in the bottom of the closet, that fit close enough, and she wore them as she padded back to the bathroom. She felt very short without her heels. The tub steamed at about half full although it was hard to tell with all the bubbles. She didn't want to waste any time waiting for the water to get deeper. She pulled off her underwear, dropped them on the floor, and stepped over the side of the tub. She couldn't help but see her scrawny self in all her naked glory as she did so. As she sank into the bubbles and hot water, she wondered if Phil liked scrawny women like her or did he like humongous breasts like Brenda's. The thought hung over her like a cloud. She didn't like the petite form she could see hiding among the bubbles in the mirror. She doubted Phil cared one whit about her. In spite of her beautiful new home here, she felt down.

Soaking in the water for an hour and a half helped her mood. After a while she gave up adding hot water every so often to keep the temperature just right in the tub. The bubbles were all gone, her fingers and toes were wrinkled like prunes and she felt like going to bed. She towelled off and put on her clean underwear. She hoped that she would be reunited with her suitcase in the morning. She put on her pyjamas and climbed into bed. She turned on the TV with the remote, and started channel surfing. She went through the channels one by one. Brenda wasn't kidding when she told her they subscribed to everything, even porn movies, which shocked and unsettled her some more. She found she wasn't in the mood to watch anything and turned it off, rolled over, and went to sleep. She didn't sleep well, in spite of her fatigue. Something didn't seem quite right and she couldn't quite put her finger on it. She wasn't worried though, she had return tickets if things didn't go as well as she hoped.

Brenda settled back down behind her desk in the lobby. Not long after a big man in jeans and a t-shirt entered from a hallway.

"Hey, babe."

"Hey, Zap. Did you watch on the monitor?"

"Sure did. Looks like our man Bernard sent us another good one. Might even be a good fit for our copper friend. Been putting a lot of pressure on us for a petite newbie like that."

"Zap, I don't have a good feeling about that request."

"Neither do I, babe. Why do you think I haven't offered one the girls that have been here for a while? This guy is a big fish and we'd best mind our business."

"Shame if she got hurt. She seems like a sweetheart."

"We don't actually know if she'll get hurt or not. Either way she is going to be a great addition."

"She did say something about meeting a man on the train she liked. It's probably nothing. Just one thing caught my attention. See that suitcase over there?"

"Yeah, what about it?"

"Go pick it up."

Zap lifted it up with a grunt and said, "What'd she bring – the whole house?"

"Not the point. She says the guy she met on the train hefted that 'like it weighed nothing'."

"Really – that's one strong son of a bitch."

Chapter III

Mark got off the subway at the Finch station. Before heading out to a nearby parking area to be reunited with his van, he decided to grab a light supper at the Tim Horton's. It meant a long wait in line because of the time of day, but Mark didn't care. He fumbled with the scrap of paper in his pocket a couple times, until his turn came. He ordered a chicken wrap, a small bowl of soup and a Boston donut for dessert. He carried it to one of the small tables by the window. Christine crossed his mind a couple of times while he observed the world passing by. He took his time. By the time he finished traffic thinned out. He yawned a couple of times. God, I'm beat he thought. Taking the train and catching up on some needed sleep didn't happen the way he planned.

From there, he made a quick stop at the grocery store to restock the fridge in the back of the van. It didn't take him long. Back at the truck he hauled open the sliding door, climbed aboard and got ready for bed.

He slept soundly for several hours, and then the nightmare that disturbed him on the train invaded his rest once again. The images swirled to life in his mind. Crispy brown, wrinkled leaves chased each other in circles without a sound down the gravel driveway past him, and disappeared into the darkness. The wind, cold and damp, moaned through the tree branches clawing at the sky. The moon, veiled by the gloom, lit his way as his basketball shoes gritted on the grey, dirty gravel of the cemetery driveway. He found himself standing in front of a small stone mausoleum. The stone door swung open, creaking on its hinges. The black interior beckoned. Mark fought the forces drawing him forward, but they carried him inside anyway. The door groaned shut trapping him. Inside a row of tables with shrouded bodies prostrate on them appeared.

He pulled back the first shroud to reveal his father's bloodless face. He lay serene and cold in death. Sam Rathman looked like an older version of Mark. The same short dark hair, the same lean, strong face, not handsome, but not ugly either. His plain face blended into crowds, a trait that served him well when he worked undercover. His eyes were much darker than Mark's. Even in death, Mark could see the strength of character, the dogged determination, the quick sense of humour, and the affection

The profound loneliness bit hard into Mark. He moved to the second table and unveiled his mother's face. He missed her. Mark had her same soft brown eyes. Even in death, though, the awful fear she must have felt just before the impact of that terrible car crash could be seen on her grey, pale features. On the third table lay his younger brother Michael. He lay as still as his father. With soft brown, wavy hair and a mischievous look about him, he didn't look like Mark at all. They always seemed to have a blast together. He died in agony, in the ambulance on the way to the hospital

He approached the fourth table trying to pull away. He knew what he would find: Nicole, her eyes open, staring at nothing, just as they had when he last saw her lying on the couch of their Montreal apartment, a trickle of dried black blood at the corner of her mouth. Guilt and anger washed over him. He then found himself standing in front of a fifth table. He pulled back the shroud and found Christine, still alive, silently begging for his help. On the other side of her, stood two figures: A round headed, black haired man, with a thick moustache, wearing a police uniform, and the other figure was a small wiry, elderly man, with a low evil laugh. The policeman pinned Christine down, while the old man pulled out a handgun and put it to her temple. She begged Mark to intervene, terror in her eyes, but he looked on powerless. He could only watch. The old man gave Mark a sneer and then pulled the trigger.

Mark awoke, his heart racing. He grabbed the clock and held it so that he could see the time: Ten to one in the morning. May as well to get to work. As he fought through the fragments of his nightmare, he remembered the note in his pocket. He ignored it.

His simple cot folded into the wall of his truck to free up space. A small table with a laptop computer on it, a stool to sit on, a small fridge, a propane powered stove, and in the very back a toilet completed Mark's man cave. Stuffed in the back of a van. He didn't mind. After a year, he was used to it.

He made his way to the back of the van to use the toilet and splash some water on his face. He usually used pubic washrooms to keep from having to dump the tank of the truck too often. It couldn't hold all that much. He got a good look at himself in the small mirror hanging on the wall back there. Lots of stubble and he looked like he'd slept on his head again. Bed head, one of his morning trademarks in college. Nicole would have taken one look at him and said it looked like it was going to be a windy day. He didn't care what he looked like. He didn't plan to see anyone, never mind someone important, and if everything went as planned, no one would see him either.

Tonight he had a mission. He picked up a new gadget built by his friend Matt. In fact, he had four of them and a few other tidbits besides. Tonight he wanted to install one of them and test it out. He crawled back to the table and seated himself on the stool. Under the table rested his small travel suitcase. He pulled it out, sat it on his lap, popped the latches and opened it up. Inside four grey boxes, with the Bell logo stamped into their fronts, nestled with wadded up newspaper between to keep them from rattling around and getting damaged. Mark lifted one out of the suitcase and put it on the table next to his laptop. He closed the suitcase and put the rest back under the table. He opened the front and drew out the two wires coiled up inside. One looked like a regular telephone jack, and the other had a small module for plugging a telephone jack. Inside the unit sat a smaller black box with a lid. Inside was a regular CD. This unit even came with a computer tone reader that would automatically record whatever numbers, were dialled. This wasn't the first time he'd tapped into phone lines to get important information, but in most cases his friend Matt made the job a lot simpler. With the Bell logo, they even looked like standard equipment to the untrained eye

Satisfied with his new toy, he got himself dressed. His travel clothes hung on a hanger, but tonight he would just dress comfortably in dark sweatpants, dark hoodie and his sneakers. Once ready, he opened the door, between the seats to the front of the van, placed his wiretap with care on the passenger side, squeezed his lank body through, and closed the door behind him. The glare of streetlights lit the parking lot. At this hour, not many people were moving about, but there were still a lot of vehicles in the lot. He turned on the ignition and flicked on his headlights. Time to do a little driving.

Mark headed for a suburb in Mississauga, to set his wiretap and be on his way. He would be able to access the calls by computer. His target's name was Serge Cote; the round headed police officer in his nightmare. Mark remembered their one and only face to face meeting from about a year and a half earlier. It seemed a lot longer than that. Mark owned a small bicycle shop in Montreal, and Serge Cote served as a police officer running the city's anti-drug unit at the time.

The day that changed Mark's whole life started with a trio of young thugs coming into Mark's store just after opening, trying to force Mark to pay up on a drug debt his former partner owed them. A tense standoff ensued. The leader of the trio, a slight, mean looking fellow whom Mark disliked the moment he laid eyes on him, wouldn't take no for an answer. Mark bought out his former partner because of the potential for this kind of trouble. He sure wasn't going to pay off some of this idiot's drug money. These thugs could happily go find his former partner and collect whatever they were owed.

The mean looking character pulled out a gun and threatened him. Mark, with one quick fluid motion relieved him of his gun, which spun halfway across the counter, and also relieved him of a great deal of his dignity. Mark regretted doing that. Had he not pissed the guy off, Nicole would still be alive. He could beat himself up over that, but it wouldn't bring her back. It didn't take too much convincing to send the trio packing after that. Mark called the police and Serge Cote showed up as the investigating officer.

Cote stood about five ten, a little on the stocky side. He had thick black hair and moustache. He gave the impression of professional competence and proved every bit as smart as he came across. Mark's father worked as a police detective before being killed in a car accident. Cote played on that fraternal connection as they chatted through the necessary paper work. Mark always thought of himself as a good judge of character so it came as quite a blow to learn the truth about Serge Cote. He worked as Francois Rodrigues' ace in the hole on the Montreal crime scene. Cote would get the drug busts, keep the competition in line and look good doing it. The Montreal branch of Rodriques' drug empire would get bigger and bigger. The only really lousy part of the arrangement for Cote was the necessity of babysitting and cleaning up after Rodrigues' not so bright nephew Rejean, who happened to be the slightly built mean character Mark had crossed swords with that morning.

Mark later relieved him of that burden but not as an intended favour. Finished with business Cote gave him a direct number to call if any further trouble developed. Mark hoped that would be the end of it. He couldn't have been more wrong. He regretted misjudging the situation. Had he known, he would have gone straight home to keep Nicole safe.

In the fall business dried up to just a trickle, so Mark decided to close up shop early and go home in the middle of the afternoon. Too much excitement for one day, besides he knew Nicole would be glad to see him. An ultrasound test a few days earlier revealed a set of twin boys in her womb. Even though she barely showed she felt exhausted all the time. Cycling home to their apartment each day gave him a good thirty minutes to think while he dodged traffic. He looked forward to the day; he would be able to move the tenants in the apartment above the store out so he and Nicole could move in. He love cycling but it just took too much time, and riding in the city really wasn't that great.

To get home quick, Mark always used a shortcut. He rode through the parking lot of an apartment building on the next street over, through a gate and a short alley into the backyard of the building he and Nicole lived in. This shortcut saved his life that day. Mark didn't know all the details of what happened but what he could piece together was that Rejean didn't accept defeat in his earlier confrontation with Mark. He and his buddies rearmed and then went to Mark and Nicole's apartment to send Mark a message. They intended to rough up Nicole real bad, maybe even rape her. Nicole resisted Rejean's assault, making him even angrier, causing him to really flip out. The roughing up went way too far and Nicole died from the injuries he inflicted. From there the gang shifted into damage control. They figured to ambush Mark, when he got home, kill him, burn the apartment, and make it look like a domestic dispute/murder-suicide, but that got derailed because Mark decided to come home early.

Expecting Mark to drive a car to the front of the building, they arranged for a look-out, which was not a very bright idea; Mark and Nicole's red Dodge Lancer was sitting in its parking spot, in full view, the whole time. Mark got almost all the way to the living room before they spotted him. The surprise saved his life. He caught a glimpse of Nicole pale, bloodied and lifeless on the couch, before diving into the bathroom. He managed to wiggle through the small window as bullets shattered the door he locked behind him. He dropped to the little porch roof over the back door and from there got to the ground. He grabbed his bike and left through the alley he just came home through.

Mark would have called 911 right away, but the clip on his cell phone busted off on his way out of the bathroom and he lost the whole thing. It probably lay in the bottom of the bathtub. He fled in full panic mode and could barely think. He knew that the people with the guns would come after him, but he had at least given them the slip for the time being. This is where Serge Cote came back into the story. Mark made a beeline for a phone booth in a nearby park. He first called 911 for help. They wanted him to stay on the line but Mark didn't think it would be safe. He didn't want to risk anyone from the gang finding him. He then called the direct line that Serge Cote gave him and told Cote everything. Cote told him to stay put and he would send help right away. After that call Mark hid himself in a thick bush right next to the phone booth. He'd stayed put, but not where anyone could see him.

A short while after he had concealed himself one of the goons that had been with Rejean at the store came snooping around the park. Mark thought about jumping him, when he got close to the bush, but kept his cool. The goon came and made a phone call. Mark could hear the entire conversation and learned an awful lot. First off this goon dialled Serge Cote and had been sent here by him. He learned Rejean Rodrigues' identity and his connection to drug lord Francois Rodrigues. Cote fumed over what had gone down, but gave instructions on the cover up. Mark would be framed for the murder of Nicole. If the law got to him first, the gang would see to it that he wouldn't live to tell his story. Mark stayed in his hiding place until it was dark and the park empty. He did a lot of thinking while he waited.

Mark drove down Dixie Road into Mississauga. Cote's new home sat in a quiet suburb there. The road at this time of the morning was virtually deserted. The old memories brought a certain amount of fresh pain. He gripped the steering wheel hard and his mouth was set in a line.

Since that day, he became a thorn in the side of Francois Rodrigues' empire. He took on his father's underworld persona and was known to his enemies as the Shadow.

His thoughts then wandered back to Christine, the girl he met on the train. Part of him yearned for the kind of companionship he shared with Nicole. It bothered him that a short period of time in the presence of an attractive young lady haunted him like this. He thought of the piece of paper in his pants pocket hanging in the back of the van. He hadn't even looked at it, but part of him wanted to. He shook the thought off. Distractions like this could get him killed.

Where would that leave the person he left behind? He knew that a survivor would feel all the pain that he lived with. She would be a complication that would be in danger, too. What if his cover got blown and they decided to try and get him through her? No, it was better this way. He shut her memory out of his mind and concentrated on the task at hand.

Mark knew where he was headed and turned off on a small residential street. He rolled through the neighbourhood and pulled to the side in front of an ordinary brick four-bedroom house. Most of the houses looked the same, but Mark made certain that he had the right one. He got out of the van with his wiretap device and a screwdriver. He installed the device right above the existing Bell phone box. Once in place, he popped open the box, disconnected the phone jack inside, plugged it into his unit, and then plugged the jack from the wiretap into the Bell box. Now all calls would be recorded. He closed everything up and took a step back. The whole set up looked like standard company equipment. He grinned to himself as he got back in the van to drive away. The whole installation took all of three minutes. He could remove it if he needed to even faster. If he had to retrieve it, there would be no evidence that it had ever been there except for some screw holes in the pole.

The mission, however, required one more step. Mark wanted to run a systems check to make sure everything functioned. He drove south again and parked in one of the major motel parking lots not far away, where he knew he could pick up a good wi-fi connection. It didn't take him long to get there. He pulled into the parking lot, found an empty spot right close to where he knew he would get the best reception, and shut down the engine. He opened the door behind the front seats and crawled back into his cave.

Once back there, he perched on his stool by the little table and powered up the laptop. He did a quick check to make sure the modem card was seated properly in its port and waited for the system to boot up. He put on the headset. He had all the time in the world, but the anticipation of completing this had him a little impatient. It seemed to take an eternity for the stupid thing to load. He sat there sitting on his hands knowing full well that if he touched any buttons while it was booting up it would only slow down the process. At long last, his desktop lit up the screen and he clicked on his Internet Explorer icon. Loading the Internet window went fast. He clicked on his favourites and went to the website that he and his friend Matt had set up for this purpose. He called up his system access page for the device he just installed. He checked the box making it active, inputted Cote's home phone number and then pushed the access calls button. It flashed for a few moments. Matt had given him a complete run down on how the system worked. When he pressed the button it would call the number and enter a code so that the wiretap would answer. In a worst case scenario, the phone in the Cote residence would ring once and then stop. Even if someone picked up the phone in the house they would not be able to hear anything because all the information would be being transmitted electronically. It was essentially a dial up Internet connection. The button stopped flashing and a voice came on his headset.

"Systems are fully functional. There are no audio files available for download," said the voice of Matt's girlfriend Marie. A nice touch Mark thought with a grin. She did a good imitation of the Bell automated system.

Mission accomplished, a new waiting game had begun. Mark hoped that Cote would cough up some valuable little bits of information. Francois Rodrigues' headquarters existed somewhere in the Toronto area. Mark deduced that much, but hadn't had any luck in finding out the location. Cote managed to swing a transfer to the Toronto Metropolitan Police force about six months ago.

Rodrigues needed him here to advance his empire. Mark followed along because of obvious reasons. Cote had no idea that Mark was tracking him. Mark felt that Cote held the key to unlocking the whole organization so that he could get at the head and finish it off. To this point he had only managed to be a pain in the ass for Rodrigues. Mark had done damage but made no progress toward the conclusion. As long as Rodrigues' empire continued Mark could never live in peace.

Christine flashed through his mind again. He had the urge to pull out her contact information. He shook off the temptation. Still he couldn't bring himself to get rid of the note. He shut down the laptop and closed the lid. Time to catch up on some sleep. He hadn't done much of that over the past few days. He climbed back into his cot and fell asleep in spite of the day's excitement.

Chapter IV

Six o'clock sharp the alarm next to Christine sounded. She gave it a semiconscious slap to kill the obnoxious buzzing. A morning person by nature, she overcame the initial confusion of waking up in an unfamiliar bed and groped around until she found the light switch. Still tired from not sleeping well, she toyed with the idea of going back to sleep for an hour, but decided against it. This eight o'clock breakfast meeting was too important, maybe the career of her dreams, she sure didn't want to risk messing it up.

Wide awake, she padded out to the kitchen. The coffee maker looked inviting and she went through the cupboards looking for coffee to put in it. Basic dishes, pots and pans and at last some instant coffee. Not the right stuff, but with a kettle and a mug, she wasn't about to start complaining. She found some packets of sugar in the same cupboard as the coffee. The fridge contained some coffee creamers; a bottle of ketchup, some mustard, an empty Brita and that was about it. After her meeting, she needed to visit the grocery store. She rinsed and filled the Brita and plugged in the kettle.

She bustled off to the bathroom while the water heated up. Checked her hair in the mirror. She had a perm and it didn't take much to put it all right. Her make up could wait till after her cup of coffee. She flashed herself her best smile and then frowned. Were they going to like her? The kettle whistle snapped her back to attention.

Back in the kitchen she prepared the coffee and carried it with her to the office, plunked herself down in front of the computer, took a few sips of coffee and sat back. The computer looked old. She pressed the power button and nothing happened. Stupid thing wasn't even plugged. After plugging it in and powering it up, it impressed her even less. Generic screen saver and three icons: Internet Explorer, My Computer and Recycle Bin. A doubt nagged at her, when the Internet wouldn't connect with anything. She laughed at herself over that. If it wasn't plugged in, why should she expect the Internet to be connected?

She sipped the last of her coffee and looked at the phone. Her thoughts went back to Phil on the train. She snorted. Way too tall for her. Still she felt so comfortable with him and safe. The way he manhandled her suitcase left her breathless. Big men like him scared her. Yet there seemed to be gentleness to him that she found appealing. Too bad she didn't expect to hear from him again. She knew he glanced at the address and phone number she gave him without looking at it. Better to forget him. He wasn't that great looking. Not only did he come off as little to aloof, his ears stuck out too much, cute superman dimple on his chin peeking through his short goatee though. Wonder what he looked like clean shaven?

With that depressing thought, she picked up the phone receiver. It was dead. What a surprise. This time the doubt hung on. She could not find a jack, where she could plug the phone into the wall. That was odd. She'd have to find out from Zap when that would be installed. Maybe she just missed it or maybe it worked through the computer somehow. If that couldn't get addressed right away, she planned to find a phone and give her mom a call later in the day. Mom wouldn't be impressed, at least not until she had something impressive to show her, but she felt guilty about taking off without saying anything. Her meeting should give her enough material to keep mom from flipping out at her.

She shifted her gaze to the window. From this high up she could see quite far. Cabbagetown lay before her. Older houses with lots of trees seemed to stretch all the way to Lake Ontario. She'd seen so much of the lake from the train yesterday that it gave her a feeling of comfort. Too bad the windows couldn't open. A whiff of air from there would be welcome.

With the caffeine starting to kick in, she dumped her coffee mug in the sink and set about getting dressed. She changed from her pyjamas back to her grey business suit. She gave it a critical look in the mirror. Compared to what Brenda wore the night before, Christine looked quite conservative. Still she thought it looked a little bit sexy on her. She also thought it gave her the air of professionalism and competence that she hoped to project. A quick brush of her teeth and a touch of makeup and she felt ready. She glanced at the clock and noted that she had more than an hour to kill yet.

She decided to pass the time exploring the bedroom. It didn't take her long. A look in the closet revealed a healthy supply of coat hangers but nothing else. The dresser drawers were half full of someone else's lingerie. She'd take the time after the meeting to bag all that up and ship it down to Brenda. She'd know what to do with it. The only other drawer with anything in it was the nightstand. There Christine found extra batteries for the TV remote control, an electric hair clipper and a lady shaver. She figured to turn the extra items there over to Brenda, as well.

At long last, she caved in and turned on the TV. As if early morning television could be described as doing something. She did her best to pay attention, anything to keep from getting nervous.

At quarter to eight a knock at the door sent Christine scrambling to answer. She checked the peephole and Brenda stood there, smiling, with some kind of cart. Christine fumbled the door open.

"Good morning, Christine. Glad to see you're all ready to go."

"Come on in... You're a bit early."

"Yeah, I thought to take the blood and urine samples before Zap got here with your suitcase. I thought you'd be more comfortable with that. We have to take the samples before you eat, anyway."

"Okay."

"Could you fill those first?" Brenda asked, wrinkling her nose as she offered to small plastic jars to Christine.

"Sure. I'll be right back."

Christine disappeared for a few minutes behind the bathroom door and then came back with the two samples.

"The blood samples are going to be less fun." While Christine was out, Brenda had put on some latex medical gloves and did a very professional job of preparing a syringe. Christine felt like she was on a visit to the doctor. A swab of alcohol on her arm, a quick jab with a needle and then several vials of blood were drawn. "I hope you don't faint like some people I've done this for."

"I've gotten light headed before but never actually fainted."

"Good. Please don't make this your first time."

"You did that well. You ever thought of being a nurse?"

Brenda smiled, "No, this is just about the extent of my medical skills."

When she finished collecting the samples, she packed up everything on the cart and wheeled it toward the door. There was a knock before she got there.

"Probably Zap with breakfast and your suitcase. I'll let him in."

Christine could see Brenda exit with the samples cart and then wheel in another cart with breakfast on it before she ever got a glimpse of Zap. She felt herself shrink back at the sight of him. He was huge. Not quite as tall as Phil but looked to be about three times as wide. She didn't ever remember seeing anyone that big before. He carried in the suitcase and dropped it with a thud and a grunt just inside the door and then shoved it to the side out of the way with his foot. He strode into the office with a rolling gait and extended his massive paw.

"Welcome to Toronto City Adventures," he rumbled

Christine rose to shake his hand and felt her hand and a good part of her forearm disappear into his grip.

"Brenda told me you were a scrawny one. You look to me like you will be a great addition to the team."

Christine smiled in response, not being able to find her voice yet. Zap wore a pale dress shirt with the neck unfastened and no tie. She might have found that unprofessional but couldn't imagine a shirt with a collar big enough for Zap's thick bull neck. His had his hair cropped short military style. His pudgy face and pug nose suited him but didn't appeal to her at all. She sensed that part of him enjoyed her obvious intimidation.

At last she managed to say, "I'm looking forward to the opportunity here."

"Good, good. Before we get down to business, it's time to eat some breakfast."

Brenda set up breakfast on the desk for everyone. Christine had several different types of cereal to choose from. Because all the boxes were open, she took a little from each box and mixed them together sprinkling granola on top before adding the milk. Zap piled what looked like a whole dozen scrambled eggs onto his plate along with his toast. The meal wasn't classy by any means but he had the table manners of a barbarian and it made her really wonder what kind of business hired her. Christine's misgivings began to build. She ate her cereal nervously. Zap asked a few questions about her family and she answered truthfully. Too frightened to ask anything herself right off, she sat with her hands in her lap between mouthfuls. Brenda chatted now and then filling up some of the dead air. Zap spoke a few times to Brenda or rather to her breasts, but that was the extent of the conversation. Christine hoped the meeting would go better once the meal finished. It didn't.

Brenda cleared Christine's desk of the plates and boxes putting everything back on the cart. Then she wheeled it out leaving Christine alone in the apartment with Zap. Brenda did not return. Christine's misgivings started to give way to fear. She wanted to make a break for the door, grab her suitcase, run downstairs, and head back home to Quebec. She might have done that, but she would have had to squeeze past Zap, who terrified her. He seemed to her fully aware of how she felt, and took his time to start to speak. His beady eyes bored into her as she fidgeted.

"This is not an interview, by the way," he finally said. "You can relax. The job is yours. The information our recruiter sent us about you is impressive enough. We have a lot of French speaking clients and the fact that you are fluent will really help us. Looking at you, I can see you are everything advertised."

Christine took that as a compliment and relaxed a little. She still found it difficult to find her voice in the face of this mountain of a man.

"How exactly will I be serving our clients?"

"You'll be entertaining clients here,"

That didn't answer her question and the word entertain kind of disturbed her in the back of her mind. Too frightened to press for clarification, she found herself tensing up again.

"I'm going to need a few pictures of you before I leave," he said, as he pulled out a small digital camera. "I want you to sit by the computer and pretend you are typing something into it."

Christine obliged and pretended to be working on a very important document. He took a few snapshots and then got a few shots of her standing by the window.

"These will do nicely," he said. "I have an important French client that we are trying to impress and would like to get a few more shots of you in some other outfit."

"My suitcase is still by the door," Christine answered. Not wanting to push past Zap who was standing in her way.

"No, no, I'm sure there are a few company uniforms stored in one of the drawers in the bedroom."

With that, he herded her into the bedroom. The word uniform baffled her just enough that she offered no resistance. He yanked open a drawer and searched for a moment.

"See I knew they were still here."

He pulled out something black and tossed it to her. She found a black negligee in her trembling hands.

"That'll do. Go ahead and put it on," he said as if it were the most normal request in the world. He moved toward the door. He wasn't giving her privacy though; he was blocking her only route of escape. Christine just stood there frozen and stared at him confused and scared.

"Well, change your clothes. I haven't got all day," he said with just a little more force in his voice.

Christine just continued to stare at him, the truth slowly penetrating through to her.

"If you don't start stripping off that business outfit of yours, I'm going to have to do it for you," he said with a great deal more menace. "I'm not going to wait much longer. I've got a lot to do today."

"I don't want the job anymore," she finally managed to squeak out. "I'll take my things and go home."

He laughed, "That isn't going to happen. We spent a great deal of money getting you here and we think you're perfect for the job. You aren't going anywhere. Now strip."

Zap smiled, as Christine's searched desperately for an escape route she knew wasn't there. He grabbed her and pinned her arms behind her back with one hand. The other massive paw started undoing buttons. Those big clammy square fingers were surprisingly nimble as her blouse yielded to his assault. His brute strength terrified her. She managed to get her arms free when he pulled her top off. She beat on him with her fists and felt the futility of it. She may as well have been beating on a concrete wall. She screamed and did everything she could to fight. He seemed to be enjoying himself as he forced her down on the bed and started pulling her skirt off. She could smell his sweat and it almost made her gag; that's when she managed to get her teeth into him. That got his attention. He stopped wrestling with her clothes and his massive hand wrapped itself around her throat and squeezed. She clawed at his arms unable to breathe. Just when she thought she would die he relaxed his grip. She gasped for breath. Gulping to fill her lungs over and over.

"You're really starting to piss me off!" he snarled. "I could kill you easier than you think. Now shut up and stop fighting me! You either let me do this or you die. Your choice."

She was terrified and stopped resisting.

"My grandmother wears sexier underwear than this," he spat.

With that, he yanked her panties down and off. All that was left of her clothes was her bra. That came off next. He physically backed off, content that she would now cooperate. She lay there naked, terrified and humiliated.

"Spread your legs apart, bitch," he growled.

She complied, certain that he would rape her. He made no move to do so though.

"I've got a lot of customers that like scrawny, skanky, titless little bitches like you, but they don't want hair down there. Hold that position," he commanded.

He pulled open the nightstand drawer. Christine shut her eyes hoping it would all just end. She didn't dare move a muscle. She heard a click and then a buzzing sound. She flinched at the sound, wishing she didn't know what it was. She flinched again, when she felt cold steel touch her pubes. Zap used the electric hair clipper to reduce her pubic hair to stubble. He then switched to the shaver until only smooth skin remained. Christine didn't move a muscle. She just endured her shame.

"You've got a nice tight little cunt on you," he commented with a deliberate leer. "Might take a break from Brenda sometime. Come up here and fuck you myself."

He paused for what seemed like an eternity.

"I'm not serious. Now open your eyes and look at me," he ordered.

He waited for her to obey, and she did, although it was obvious she wanted to continue ignoring him until he went away.

"This electric razor is stored in the drawer here. It is yours. I expect you to use it to keep that cunt of yours smooth. I will personally come and check daily to make sure it's been done. If it isn't, I will do it for you and possibly think of some punishment for you. Do you understand?"

He waited for her to nod her head yes, which she finally did. Then he ordered her to model a few item of lingerie while he took a few more snapshots. He took pictures until he had what amounted to a soft porn shoot. Then Zap put everything away and left Christine to herself.

Christine sat in the middle of the bed near the head hugging her knees for most of the morning crying off and on. She went over everything in her mind blaming herself for being stupid. She realized only Phil knew her whereabouts and that assumed he took the time to look at the note before throwing it away. Some guy she didn't know. If he called the number she gave him, or even came to the address, she believed they would tell her there was no such person here. Probably would tell him nobody fitting her description ever came there. She figured to call her parents, when she got settled in Toronto, after starting her new job. She felt sick. She felt scared, alone and hopeless.

After crying till she had nothing left to cry she started looking around her prison. She became aware that close to the ceiling on the wall on each end of the room small web cam type cameras watched her. She felt vulnerable aware of how little she wore. Zap left her in a g-string. She hated it, but didn't dare move yet. She finally pulled one of the blankets off the bed and wrapped herself in that. She felt only a little better.

Finally she got up and made her way to the bathroom. On her way, she noticed the little web cams in all the rooms even the bathroom. She shuddered when she saw herself in the mirror. She saw the terror in her red-rimmed eyes. The skin on her throat showed a large handprint still a little red from where Zap had gripped her. She thought she looked hideous. She fought back a renewed surge of tears. She didn't go back to the bedroom determined to get to know every inch of her prison. If any way out existed she was going to find it. Even as the thought went through her mind, she recognized the hopelessness of it. Still it buoyed her flagging spirits a little.

Early in the afternoon the door to her apartment opened again and in walked Zap. She shrank into a corner of the office at the sight of him. He brought her food to eat, which he left on the desk. He ordered her to eat it, but made no attempt to approach her. He didn't stick around. He left almost as quickly as he came. She waited, curled up in a ball in the corner for fifteen minutes, until she thought he wasn't coming back for a while. She knew that they were watching though. She could feel eyes on her. She dared to get up to check things out. She bypassed the prepared sandwiches, she was supposed to eat, and grabbed the strap from her suitcase. She dragged it into the bedroom, tipped it over, and opened it right on the floor. She went through everything to make sure nothing was missing. She again felt like eyes bored into her from the little web cams around the apartment. She pulled the blanket a little tighter around her. She wanted to get into her clothes again but she didn't want to expose herself to whoever was probably watching her.

She had an idea. She went to the office, got one of the chairs that didn't have wheels, and brought it to the bedroom. She stood on that to hang one of her t-shirts on each of the web cams. Then she changed out of the g-string and into a comfortable pair of her own underpants. It relieved her not to have that awful string scraping back and forth between her butt cheeks. She put on her pink sweat suit, fuzzy socks and a comfortable bra.

She wanted to leave the web cams covered and just hideout in the bedroom, but she knew that this would lead to Zap coming back and she didn't even want to think about what might come with that. She climbed back up on the chair and retrieved her clothes. She stored everything in her suitcase. Somehow moving her things to the dresser drawers and closets wasn't something she wanted to do. She did not want to stay here and if the chance presented itself, she would be out that door with her things in a heartbeat, even if she had to drag everything all the way down the stairs by herself.

She then remembered lunch waited for her on her desk. She wasn't terribly hungry; in fact, under the circumstances; she would have happily starved herself. The problem is Zap made it very clear that she should eat, so that she wouldn't lose weight. He didn't want her to become any scrawnier. She dragged the chair she borrowed with her on her way back to the little office. Chicken sandwich, lettuce, tomato and just the right amount of mayonnaise, they even took the time to toast the bread. It tasted good and made her feel better even though she wouldn't admit it. She decided to spend the rest of the day watching the television. It distracted her mind from her current predicament. This way she wouldn't have to think about her new life. She figured to get some "job training", which meant Zap, and meant learning firsthand how she would be entertaining clients. Just the thought nauseated her.

Chapter V

Mark woke up in the middle of the morning well rested. Work tended to pile up, whenever he travelled. Maintaining the lives of his various personas challenged his physical limits at times. If he didn't do it, the facades could collapse, exposing a chink in his armour. They all lived at different addresses, whether those places really existed or not, had jobs whether they existed or not and bank accounts. Most of it ran automatically, but Mark did have to monitor things and when necessary step in to keep up the facades. He mentally thanked his late father for the genius of it all. This would keep him busy until well in to the afternoon. Then he would need to become Phil again, because Phil worked a real job, maintained a real address in Brampton, and his real boss expected him back after a week of vacation from delivering pizzas.

Mark wasn't delivering pizzas for the money. Every trail he followed to find Rodrigues' lair led here. Rodrigues owned a number of apartment buildings in the area, and one in particular seemed to be a focal point of the organization's activity. Every month or so, the important people in Rodrigues' organization in the Toronto area would come to this building and then disappear. They would reappear here later and then go about their business. Mark delivered pizzas to customers in this building for four months and he couldn't figure it out. He managed to visit every floor in the building – by accident, if necessary – including, at least twice, the basement and had found nothing but residential units, nothing out of the ordinary. He thought maybe they were changing vehicles here and then going to another location, but he'd hid himself outside and no vehicles came out that might be doing that. He sensed that the answer must be right in front of him, and fumbled for the key that would unlock it. Consistently his best lead came in the person of Serge Cote. Frustration and impatience ate at him. He knew better than to give in to the feeling.

"Phil" lived in a small basement apartment just north of Steeles Avenue tucked behind the businesses lining that road. A great location for his purposes, it sat close to his target and within easy walking distance of Pizza Pizza, for whom he delivered. His employer didn't even know he owned a vehicle. The subcompact he used for deliveries gave him a crick in the neck after a long drive, but it was easy to park, and manoeuvred really well in heavy traffic. He actually excelled at the job. Rocco, the boss, liked him, the customers liked him and he had not yet failed to deliver a pizza on time. The pay up front sucked, but if the customer liked you the tips really added up. While he didn't actually need the cash, this cover currently supported the entire operation, without Mark needing to transfer any money from somewhere else.

Mark parked the truck in his parking spot and headed for the door on the side of the building that led to the basement. A very clean, well-maintained little apartment greeted him, having a large all-purpose room, which served as living room, dining room, and tucked in the corner a small kitchenette. A small bathroom with a shower and a small bedroom completed the layout. Mark rarely spent any time there so it stayed immaculately clean with little effort. Today's visit would be brief; just long enough to shower, shave and trim his moustache and goatee. He took the time to do his laundry, too. The dress pants were dry clean only, so he left them in the truck. He again suppressed a passing thought to look at the note with Christine's phone number and address. He started to think maybe he should dispose of it, so it wouldn't keep crossing his mind and tempting him. He couldn't quite bring himself to do that though. After work, he would see if Cote's phone line would yield anything interesting. He wasn't expecting too much but you never know.

Zap kicked back in his office. The morning went quite well. Christine laying the chompers on his shoulder came as a bit of a surprise though. She bit him hard enough to draw blood. He sniggered at the thought of going for rabies shots. He knew he scared the crap out of her, but even though she behaved after that, he knew she wasn't broken. He glanced at the surveillance monitor but he finished observing her. He switched to the hallway camera. He already knew enough from watching her earlier.

She actually impressed him some. In spite of appearances, the little bitch proved a lot more intelligent and tougher mentally than she looked. Understanding her situation she quickly noticed the monitoring equipment. When she blocked them, he started getting concerned, but she uncovered them again obviously, wanting a little privacy to change her clothes. She kept her clothes packed though and he figured she would leave if half an opportunity presented itself. She went over the apartment carefully looking for some flaw in her prison. She tried the doorknob a couple times. She even went to the kitchen to pick up something and then she spent some more time trying to monkey with the door catch. She concealed efforts from the monitors, but it was obvious to him that she carried a thin knife out of the kitchen and tried to poke around between the door and the doorpost. For a country girl, she sure had some street smarts about her. Fortunately for him the lock mechanism design defeated that kind of break in or, in this instance, break out. Her blood tests wouldn't come back till tomorrow. It amused him some that he could get those test results faster than a hospital could. He already knew what the results would be from experience. This girl would be clean as a whistle.

He had a pang of regret. Petite and pretty, she would have been a terrific addition to his stable of girls. No, she wasn't his type but a lot of clients really liked girls like her. She had an air of innocence about her, which even he thought a turn on. Unfortunately, he had been under a great deal of pressure from his superior to produce a girl fitting her basic description. Tanya and Michelle fit, but he didn't want to offer either of them up for the type of client he suspected this big shot in the organization was. Why else would they pay him that kind of money up front and tell him he was expected to clean up afterward and keep his mouth shut. Whatever party girl he provided would likely be a mess when this guy finished with her.

Zap had his own sense of honour, right or wrong, twisted as it might be. Yes, he enjoyed breaking a recruit down and then training her to take care of the customers. Through the process, though, he got attached to the girls, and once they were ready to work he took care of them. Just a couple of weeks earlier, one of the clients got a little rough with one of the girls and Zap had personally made sure that wouldn't happen again. The asshole didn't listen too well and Zap beat the crap out of him.

Luckily for him, this job didn't require she get any training. No risk of him developing protective feelings for her. He would contact the customer after the blood test results came in and make him an offer. Probably send him some pictures. Zap hoped the customer wouldn't like what he saw and then he could train this slut to be one of his regulars. Deep down though he knew Christine would catch this customer's fancy and be sacrificed. Too bad, he thought for just a second before putting it out of his mind. If he couldn't do that he wouldn't have a job very long. Might even wake up dead. Sentimentality could be fatal in this business.

A few days later Christine felt caged, still going stir crazy in her apartment. Zap only visited her once a day, which was more than enough. True to his word he checked to make sure she used the electric razor. He gave her a second round of hands on instruction on the subject. She made sure he wouldn't have to put her through that again, thankful at least that she hadn't been raped...yet. Brenda brought her food, collected her laundry and talked only a little. The TV remained her main companion and that really wasn't a whole lot of fun. She prayed now and then, hopelessly, that somehow someone would come and rescue her from all this. She assumed her "training" had not yet begun, because they were waiting for her blood test results to show she wasn't carrying some dread STD. She didn't want to think about the future. It frightened her too much.

She dreamt the night before that Phil came and let her out of the apartment. He carried her enormous suitcase down the stairs with ease. They sneaked out the front door with Brenda and Zap snoring away in the lobby. He drove her to the airport and they flew off to the Caribbean or some island somewhere. They were alone together and he told her he loved her. The dream had been wonderful until he took her in his arms and turned into Zap while they were kissing. She had a good cry in the middle of the night over that.

She settled herself down on the bed to watch the television, flipping through the guide trying to find something interesting to watch. She wasn't much for sports or soap operas so even with hundreds of channels she found the search for something remotely interesting a challenge. She noticed that the show "America's Most Wanted" just started. She punched in the channel number with the amused thought that maybe she would see a clip on her employer. What she saw, when she got there, shocked her more. A younger picture of a clean-shaven Phil splashed across the screen. She couldn't deny the evidence staring her in the face. Only his name wasn't Phil it was Mark Rathman. He was wanted in Canada for the murder of his wife and in connection with the death of some underworld character named Rejean Rodrigues.

The story of her cousin's murder flooded back into her memory. Aunt Yvette moved to California as a young adult to try to make it in the movies. She married some small time crook that spent most of his time in jail. From that time, most of the rest of the family shunned her. Christine never met her or her daughter Nicole. She heard oftentimes about what awful people they were growing up. Especially whenever she expressed a desire to see the world beyond the townships where she grew up.

When Nicole's murder sent shockwaves through the family, her Mom got on her back over every loser date she brought home, reminding her that if she got involved with the wrong people awful things like that might happen to her. The news sucked almost all the hope out of her. Maybe Mom knew what she preached to her about after all. Maybe she should have listened more. She blamed herself again for her current situation. This Mark Rathman character she met who called himself Phil seemed like the perfect man. Part of her didn't want to believe it; since leaving home, her whole social life consisted of pimps, hookers and murderers. Her spirits sank.

She listened numbly to the whole clip on Mark. His father worked as a special police investigator in Niagara Falls and made quite a name for himself. Mark's family died tragically, in a car accident, around the time he graduated from high school. They were apparently cut off in traffic, lost control, and crashed into a bridge abutment along the QEW.

Mark, a promising young athlete, went to University in California, where he played basketball and participated in several other sports. His athletic career petered out by the time he graduated. He met and married Nicole while touring California by bicycle shortly after earning a Bachelor's Degree. They eventually settled in Montreal to be close to Nicole's family. Christine remembered the news, that Aunt Yvette moved back to Quebec, when her crook husband died of cancer. The only member of the family that welcomed her back was her Grandfather, who in spite of the evidence also seemed convinced of Mark's innocence. Mark opened a bicycle shop in Montreal along with another distant relative as a partner. Mark later bought him out and life apparently looked up. The report revealed that the couple welcomed the news of Nicole's pregnancy just days before the murder.

The show could not explain why he suddenly turned into a monster and attacked his wife, then tried to cover everything up by setting the building on fire and running off. The TV program concluded by advising listeners not to approach or try to apprehend Mark, because he not only carried an array of weapons, but also had impressive martial arts skills. There were apparently several reliable sightings of him in Florida. That drew a snort from Christine. He wasn't in Florida. She'd seen him right here in Toronto out of her life and probably for the better. She found it hard to believe that things could be worse than they were though. He didn't seem dangerous to Christine at all. She felt completely safe with him on the train

The news weighed heavily on Christine. She turned off the TV to have herself a good cry. While she sat there crying an awful thought struck her. Maybe Mark worked for the same people who were holding her captive. Maybe he was on the train to escort her to these awful people to make sure she got there. Hopelessness washed over her.

Chapter VI

Mondays were always slow for pizza deliveries and Mark got let off early. He took the time to go over the phone calls that he downloaded from his wiretap. Most of the calls featured Mrs. Cote calling and talking to her friends. Serge made a shrewd career move in marrying this diminutive woman, from a wealthy well to do family. She despised him, though, and living with this shrew couldn't have been much fun. If Serge had not been such a bastard himself, Mark might have felt sorry for him. Mark fast-forwarded through those calls. No sense listening to all that garbage. Good thing his wiretap had several gigs of memory. She sure had no trouble expressing herself. After some patient searching, he found a call for Serge himself.

"Hey Cote. How's it going? This is Zap. I got some good news you've been waiting for."

"I'm listening."

"By the way, thanks for getting rid of that turkey Marv Lindsay. I haven't seen him staking out the place for more than two weeks now."

Mark grinned. Marv Lindsay had to be the world's worst undercover operator in the history of police work. Had this Dick Tracy look about him. Mark knew him well because he had partnered with his father, Sam Rathman for most of his career. Besides being his father's closest friend, he had redeeming qualities of his own as a police officer. Calm and easygoing, people on both sides of law confided information to him. Lindsay's calm façade belied intelligence and sheer tenacity. He had a knack for sticking with baffling cases, putting all the facts together and solving it. His bumbling in the field often turned into an asset as he often got underestimated.

"No problem, I'm his superior and I just told him to stop wasting his time staking out your place and find something useful to do. I threatened to make his life miserable if he didn't. Could you get to the point though? I'm a busy man."

Mark doubted if dissuading Lindsay could be as easy as that, but the fact remained that there had been no stake out car for better than two weeks. Zap would have seen him.

"Look Cote, I think I have a new girl you would be interested in, if you catch my meaning."

The blood in Mark's veins froze at that. He knew that Cote visited Rodrigues' whorehouses now and then. Most of the time he went on the spur of the moment. He would then have his recreation and go home. Special arrangements meant something more and a knot formed in Mark's stomach at the thought.

"Real petite and innocent looking, saving her just for you, no clients no training, I can send you pictures by email."

Mark felt a chill run up his spine and the hairs on the back of his neck stand up. His aroused suspicions set up a huge conflict within him. He tailed Serge Cote hoping to be led to Rodrigues and a way to shut the whole organization down forever proved tedious boring work. He covered his tracks well.

Mark, however, stumbled across this same scenario in Montreal once. It had been a special arrangement for Cote: a new girl with no experience for him to do as he pleased with. Mark found her corpse the following day in a dumpster, naked, beaten almost beyond recognition and then strangled. The sight of her lifeless abused body made him ill. Cote was a monster. Mark wanted to do the world a favour and kill him, but that would have to wait because Mark needed Cote to lead him to Rodrigues. Now this was playing out in front of him again. Could he sit idly by while another innocent woman lost her life to this monster? He knew the answer to that. He just hoped he wouldn't be too late. The image of Nicole's lifeless body flashed by in his mind and then Christine's image appeared in place of the corpse in the dumpster. A horrible thought crossed his mind. He wished he had just killed the bastard back then. He had given an anonymous tip to the police in Montreal. Cote had to put in a hell of a lot of overtime to cover for himself that time. If this had happened since, they had been more careful about disposing of the bodies.

"Yeah, send me the pictures but give me more details right now."

"Okay, okay. She's a petite blond just five feet tall. Came to us by train late last week from out in Quebec. Just like you. Speaks French. If you want to, you could cuss her out in French..."

Both men laughed at that, but Mark wanted to be sick. His horrid thought moved toward reality. He had to know for sure. He paused the recording and pulled his dress pants off the hanger they hung from and pulled out the piece of paper she wrote on. Just as he feared the phone number and the address matched Zap's business. He cursed himself for not having looked at it earlier. No woman pursued a secretarial position at this address. He could have saved her the horrors that she had already gone through and from the ones that were to come. He had to act there was no time to waste.

He fast-forwarded through the recorded messages not caring what they said. He just needed to know if Cote was going to follow up on this and when. The first call had been Sunday during the day, yesterday. He found the follow up call that evening. As he feared, Cote was interested and an appointment had been set for Monday at nine o'clock just a little after dark. He cursed when he looked at the clock. It showed eight thirty and he wouldn't get there before things started. He threw the truck in gear, and vowed he would try to get there anyway. He hoped that Cote engaged in a lot of verbal abuse and posturing before he really went to work. Problem was he didn't know.

He cursed the normal traffic in frustration all the way there. He was grateful to be already dressed for action because he dared not waste any time. So much for planning a careful operation, he only had time for improvisation. His mind raced trying to work out the fastest way to access the building and find Christine. The only weapons on his person were a couple of throwing knives in a pouch between his shoulder blades, his favourite k-bar and double end daga hidden at his waist.

It would have been nice to have a gun with him, but the one he had sat buried under some stuff in the back and Mark couldn't waste time searching for it. He groped behind the seat while he drove searching through his private medicine cabinet. Not everything in that cabinet was legal and soon his hand closed on a bottle of tranquilizer. He transferred that to the seat beside him and continued his groping search. When he found some hypodermic needles, he knew he was in business. At a stoplight, he filled several of them and put them in a fanny pack he used cycling. He strapped it around his waist with one hand, while he steered with the other. He then pulled his shirt over it. This would be a blessing for anyone unfortunate enough to get in his way. He didn't like busting people up if he didn't have to.

He parked just around the corner from his target and leaped out of the driver's seat onto the sidewalk. The time on the dashboard clock said ten minutes after nine. Mark sprinted to the front door. Brenda and Zap chatted in the lobby, too absorbed in each other to notice Mark's arrival. Mark gave the glass door a frantic knock and waved to get their attention. He looked like any idiot on the street. Zap came to the door not looking happy.

"Get lost asshole. We aren't open."

"Hey, I got a flat tire. Need to borrow a phone to call a garage."

Zap decided to unlock and open the door to better get his point across. Seizing the moment, Mark ripped the door open wide and slammed a surprised Zap backwards into the lobby. Brenda stood rooted in place, disbelief written on her face, as Mark's rapid-fire assault of fists and feet had Zap helpless on the floor in seconds. Mark jabbed the needle into Zap. Brenda scrambled for a gun they kept in the desk drawer only to have Mark snatch it away ahead of her.

"Thanks, I collect these." He flipped on the safety catch and stuffed the gun into his waist of his pants. He then grabbed her chin and forced her to look him right in the eyes. She tried to look away, not being used to having men look her in the face.

"I don't intend to hurt you if I don't have to," he said in a dead calm tone. "There's a pretty little blond here who had a special appointment at nine. Do you know what I'm talking about?"

She found herself unable to speak but she understood and she nodded yes.

"Where is she?"

She managed to squeak out, "She's in the basement room with her customer."

"Take me there now," he commanded.

Brenda led the way to the stairs. She wore a very tight skirt and high stilettos. Mark chaffed at the slow speed of it all, but he followed. They descended the stairs and then started down the hall, Brenda's heels clicking on the concrete floor. She pulled out a bunch of keys and they started rattling, as well. That was enough for Mark. He put a hand over her mouth a put a knife to her throat.

"Not a sound. Understood?" he hissed in her ear. "This bastard gets no warning."

She nodded and they then proceeded without the noise. The door at the end of the hall had a privacy glass window in it and Mark could see a shadow moving on the other side of it. Muffled grunts, thuds and curses came from inside the room. It only took Mark a few seconds to size up the door. With one tremendous kick, it flew open inward and then bounced back. Mark bulled his way into the room.

Cote didn't stand a chance. The doorknob caught him in the hip and Mark slammed him to the floor before Cote even saw his attacker. Since he was dressed only in a shirt, Mark was able to jab the needle into bare flesh. Cote's world swam before his eyes a moment and then he slipped into unconsciousness. The room smelled of vomit.

While Mark disabled her tormentor, Christine retreated to the far corner of the room, where she cowered, naked, whimpering and shaking. Christine arms, legs, back and buttocks were covered with welts from the belt still wielded by the unconscious Cote. Mark hurried over to her and then rubbed her shoulder where there was no obvious injury. He spoke to her as if speaking to a frightened child.

"I am so sorry, Christine. If I'd looked at the address you gave me I would have never let you come here."

The whimpering sound subsided, surprising Mark. She seemed to be responding to him. He figured by her condition she would be responding only by instinct. "Look I have to get you out of here and bring you somewhere safe. Can you try to stand up?"

She surprised him again as she wobbled to her feet. He got an arm around her to support her and then turned to Brenda who stood at the door wide eyed, gaping in horror.

"Give me the bastard's coat so this girl can have a little dignity," he ordered

When Mark turned, Brenda caught a glimpse of Christine's face. An ugly gash above her almost swollen shut left eye oozed blood. Her nose bled, as well, and her mouth looked distorted from swelling on that side of her face.

"Oh my God, what did he do to you?" Brenda said in complete horror, as she handed over the coat.

Mark managed to get the coat wrapped around her and then noticed her eyes glazing as her knees buckled under her. The arm he had around her kept her from falling back to the ground. He hoisted her now unconscious body on to his shoulder and carried her out. Brenda cooperated at this point and did her best to open doors in their path.

"Anything I should do to help?" she asked, scurrying to keep up with Mark's long strides.

"You willing to donate a little blood?" he asked.

Brenda looked at him confused.

Mark explained, "The people you work for won't be happy with you if it looks like you cooperated with me, at all. If I put a scratch on your throat you can tell them I forced you. Then you can delete any pictures of this girl out of your computers and if you have access, destroy the security camera tapes for the building."

"Promise me it won't leave a scar and I'll do it."

Mark gave her the scratch and they continued on into the lobby.

"By the way," she added, "Zap brought Christine's suitcase and purse downstairs before you came. He planned to move her to a different room afterwards."

"Great, I'll take them with." he responded, surprised at this one stroke of luck. "When you're done deleting pictures, I want you to call whatever emergency line you have. I don't want you to get yourself into trouble."

Brenda opened the door for Mark and as he went out the door he said, "Tell them I called myself The Shadow."

Mark hurried toward his van around the corner. He stumbled on the curb and twisted his ankle. He swore but kept going. He put the suitcase down when he got to the van so he could open the sliding door then he carefully laid Christine down on his cot. She was drifting in and out of consciousness.

"Hold it right there mister, this is the police," said a familiar voice.

Good grief, thought Mark, Lindsay still staked the place out, but on foot from the bushes. Then he realized this might be a good thing.

"Keep your hands where I can see you and back out of the truck." Lindsay ordered.

Mark complied. Moving slowly.

"That's it take your time. Now turn around so I can have a look at you," Lindsay commanded again.

Mark turned, "Marv Lindsay!"

Lindsay's jaw dropped open in recognition.

"My Dad told me you were a medic in the forces before you became a police officer. That girl in there needs you to look at her. I need to know if she has to see a real doctor."

"Mark Rathman, I haven't seen you since you went to college. I'm supposed to arrest you on sight you know."

Mark grinned, "You aren't going to though are you."

Lindsay holstered his gun with a shrug, "Judging by the way you handled Zapparoli back there I doubt I could. Let's have a look at your girlfriend."

Lindsay climbed into the truck as Mark made way for him. He wasn't prepared for what he saw though.

"My God, Mark! She's had the living crap beat out of her. Did you kill the bastard who did this?"

"I sure wanted to. Wanted to make it hurt too, but no, he's still alive but he won't be doing this for a while."

"It wasn't Zap, was it?" Lindsay continued.

"Naw, you know him better than that. He takes care of his girls in his own way," Mark answered.

"Who was it?" Lindsay asked not giving up.

"I can't tell you. Can you examine while I'm driving because I made a great deal of trouble in there before I left and the shit is going hit the fan at any time. We need to get out of here."

"Drive on but I'm not done asking questions," answered Lindsay.

Mark slammed the sliding door shut, hobbled around and got behind the wheel. He pulled away trying not to jostle the passengers. He opened the door to the back so he could talk back and forth.

"There's a big first aid kit full of medical supplies right behind my seat," Mark offered helpfully.

Lindsay heard him, but didn't reply. Christine had regained consciousness and he was focusing on the task at hand. He carefully checked for internal injuries and checked for broken bones. The bleeding had for the most part stopped. He spoke in low tones and Mark only heard snippets of what was being said over the sound of the engine. He did hear him ask her if she had been raped. He didn't hear her reply but from what Lindsay said after that seemed to indicate that Cote hadn't gotten that far yet, when Mark spoiled his fun

Well away from that part of town, Mark pulled the truck into a parking lot and joined the pair in the back. Christine still looked pretty bad even though Lindsay had carefully cleaned away the dried blood and vomit. Christine lay awake and in obvious pain.

"Thanks for taking me out of there Mark," she whispered.

"Sorry I didn't really look at your note before I put you in that cab," Mark replied with some regret.

Mark turned to Lindsay a hint of anger in his eyes. "Why'd you tell her my name?"

"Not me," said Lindsay, eyebrows raised. "Now don't go grillin' her over that because I'm not quite done here. Gotta shave her eyebrow so that I can close this gash with those butterfly bandages you have. Didn't want to try that bumping along down the road."

Lindsay worked carefully and quickly and soon the gash was held tightly closed.

"There," he said with some satisfaction. "Should heal up with almost no scar. She needs rest though. Do you have any pain killers?"

"Sure," Mark said, "Over here."

He pulled open another small cabinet. He handed a small bottle of pills to Lindsay who examined the label

"These'll put her to sleep," he observed. "That's one hell of a stash you got there. Looks like you knocked off a whole pharmacy. Looks like your housekeeper has been on a long vacation too."

Christine gasped in pain and winced as they helped her sit up so she could swallow the pills with a gulp of water. Helping her lay back down again drew further gasps. She winced with every small movement.

"Let's give her some peace and get in the front," Mark said. "I'm sure she doesn't need to be bothered by us anymore."

Christine drifted off to sleep as the two men made their way to the front of the van. They closed the door behind them.

"How bad is she hurt?" Mark asked, before he even started the motor.

"If I had my druthers she'd be in a hospital with an IV in her and a staff of competent nurses looking after her, but she hasn't got anything that can't be cared for safely at home."

"I want a rundown top to bottom," Mark insisted.

"Everything she has is superficial except for three cracked ribs. She threw up when he kicked her in the stomach but amazingly there are no signs that any internal organs are damaged. No loose teeth just that ugly cut and a lot of bruising virtually everywhere."

"So if I care for her she'll recover completely."

"Yes. She is going to be really miserable for the first week because it is going to hurt with every breath she takes. After that it'll get better. Emotionally she is pretty tough. Thankfully the bastard didn't rape her."

Mark nodded, "Wish I'd gotten there sooner."

"So who is the bastard who did this?" Lindsay asked again.

"I know you well enough not to tell you," Mark answered. "This is my war. Besides, you'll figure that much out on your own soon enough."

Lindsay looked at him long and hard and then spoke. "So this whorehouse is part of Francois Rodrigues' empire."

Mark nodded yes.

"Our piece of shit must be someone real high up in the organization and you've been tailing him hoping to be led to the top so you can bring the whole thing down," Lindsay paused with eyebrows raised.

"Very good," Mark remarked

Lindsay continued, "The little sweetheart in the back there is a complication. You knew something horrible was going to happen to her unless you intervened and you couldn't help yourself. Only you got there too late."

"Oh. I wasn't too late," Mark said his mouth set in a grim line. "I found what was left of the last one in a dumpster. He was just getting warmed up."

Lindsay looked bothered at that. "Evil bastard. You know I really want to know who he is."

"Best I can do is give you some instructions," Mark said. "Before I drop you off, Rodrigues has eyes in the police force here in Toronto. Zap knew you were staking his place out. That's why you got orders to layoff. They know this mess was my doing. They know you worked with my Dad and they will think you are helping me. Trust me, they will be coming to talk to you and you have I figure a day and a half to think up a really good alibi for tonight."

"How'd you know I was ordered to stay away?" Lindsay asked.

Mark grinned, "I have my sources. Just don't go back. If I'd had time to do an infrared scan tonight I would not have been surprised to see you. If they're convinced you were out there and saw anything, your life might not be worth a plug nickel."

Lindsay looked at Mark and nodded, "It's going to be real difficult not to start my own investigation you know."

"They're going to be watching you very closely," Mark warned. "Remember what they did to my family when they thought Dad was getting close. You and I both know that it was not an accident. You don't want that sort of thing to happen to you and June do you? Besides, I actually might need your help when I crack this and I want you to still be around to give that help."

Lindsay paused long and thought hard, "Okay I'll play by your rules. It won't be easy but it makes sense."

Mark was relieved. This whole operation was reckless from top to bottom. He didn't have a choice though unless you consider allowing a young lady to be beaten, raped and killed an acceptable choice. He knew the fallout from this would haunt him for a long time. He had to consider his long undercover surveillance of Cote no longer a secret. Phillip Brock as a cover stood a good chance of exposure. Finally, to deal with the problem called Christine sleeping in the back of the van. What the hell was he going to do with her now that he rescued her? He couldn't send her home because Cote would be sure to grab her there. The only option available was to keep her with him for the time being. Oh, well what's done is done. He just had to keep playing this one as it came.

"I don't know how close I am to cracking this case, Marv. The girl and I are going to have to lay low for a while. At least until she heals up and the dust settles."

"How will I be able to get into contact with you?" Lindsay asked.

"You won't," Mark said as he pulled the van to the curb in front of an older suburban house. "As you can see I know where you live."

Lindsay laughed, "You are just like your Dad."

He gave Mark an affectionate slap on the leg before getting out of the truck. "You're alright. I really miss playing cops and robbers with your Dad. Sam and I shared a lot of good times. Take care of yourself," and with a wink, "and your little complication back there."

"Just don't go looking for trouble and maybe we'll see each other again," Mark said as he gave a wave good bye.

Chapter VII

Mark knew he had work to do before Cote and Zap regained their senses and reorganized, so he wasted no time. Christine doped up on pain killers would sleep for hours anyway, so she wasn't an immediate concern. He hoped the cot would be comfortable enough for her when the painkillers wore off. He drove straight to Cote's home in Mississauga. When he got there he got out of the truck, screwdriver in hand, and removed his wiretap device. Kind of sad, he thought. He originally expected to keep it in place for months. Paid for itself, though. After rubbing some dirt into the screw holes, he tossed the unit onto the passenger seat of the truck, and made his escape. He didn't expect Cote and company to sort through the chaos he created for a couple days, but they would eventually and by that time he better have made himself scarce. His ankle throbbed. It wasn't a bad sprain, but he had trouble keeping it loose, and it began hampering his mobility. No time to worry about that.

He made a detour on the way back to Brampton. He had a small cargo trailer squirreled away and he figured he could get his small apartment of stuff loaded before daybreak before anyone woke up in the neighbourhood and noticed him. There wasn't that much stuff; he packed it up in a hurry like this before.

He picked up the trailer and parked by Phil's apartment a few minutes after midnight. With his ankle hampering him, the double bed mattress and box springs were a challenge. He loaded them first and felt some satisfaction that he'd managed it without disturbing the people living upstairs. The rest proved easier. The bed frame and his desk, which was the only other significant pieces of furniture, broke down for transport. Hastily, he packed the food in the fridge, and all his other belongings into Rubbermaid boxes and stacked them in the trailer. Before sunrise he busied himself wiping down the inside of the now empty apartment. With day break approaching he still needed more time to finish but he knew he had to move the truck and trailer right away or risk being noticed.

Mark started up the motor and idled his way onto the street. No one saw him at all. He didn't drive far. He pulled into the big parking lot at the Bramalea City Centre shopping mall. They would be invisible there. He closed up the van and, with some discomfort, walked back to the apartment to finish wiping everything down. In case he compromised his cover, he did not want a single fingerprint left when he finished. The ankle loosened up as he walked and soon it wasn't bothering him anymore. He knew he would pay for that later. When he got there he wiped down the rest of the apartment within an hour. He wasn't afraid his enemies would come to look for him that soon, but he did fear the painkillers helping Christine sleep would wear off before he got back. While he wiped everything down his ankle tightened up again. He called Rocco and left him a message that he had a family emergency to attend to. Advised him that he wasn't sure when he would be back. He unplugged the phone, tucked it under his arm and made his exit wiping the doorknobs as he left. All the way back to the van he worried he would find a disoriented, frightened and sore Christine. The thought distracted him from the pain in his swollen ankle until it loosened up again from the long walk.

To Mark's relief, when he got back she still slept. Couldn't be too long before the pain would wake her up. He needed sleep himself, but he wanted to make sure her needs were addressed before he did that. He also needed to get his ankle elevated and put some ice on it, but doing that with Christine in his bed was going to be a real challenge. The back of even a large van has its limits. He managed to lie down on the floor squeezed between the bed and the desk with his foot up on the stool with an ice pack on it.

Christine wasn't awake yet before he realized this wasn't working too well. He stayed like that because he couldn't think of any other possible solution for the time being.

After about thirty minutes, she awoke.

"Mark?" she called in a thin weak voice.

"Right here," came the reply, muffled underneath the cot. Mark struggled to a sitting position so that she could see him.

"Feel any better?" he asked.

"Worse," she answered. "I really have to go to the bathroom."

"I have a toilet in the back there. I can help you if you need it."

"I'll manage," she said, not believing she could.

She winced as she sat up and then managed to crawl to the toilet. Mark drew the curtain he installed, but never used before to give her some privacy. She lingered back there for quite a while. Mark rummaged through her suitcase and found some clean underwear, which he passed around the curtain to her. She took them gratefully and put them on in spite of the agony she suffered.

"What else do you want to wear?" he asked.

"There's a pink pyjama in there. I don't think I'm going to do much more than lay in bed."

"Okay I see them."

Mark passed them around the curtain, as well. Awhile later she crawled back to the cot and lay back down exhausted from the effort. The effects of the painkiller had by now passed and she winced noticeably with every breath.

"Hurts pretty bad, doesn't it? Did you want some more painkiller right now?"

"You could have rescued me just a little sooner," she said. She meant it as a joke, but it didn't come across that way.

"I'm so sorry. I'm going to regret not looking at the paper you gave me when you handed it to me for a long time. I would not have let you go there?" he answered his voice tinged with guilt.

"You didn't really want to see me again. Did you?" It pained her to say it but she knew the truth of it.

"No, I didn't," he admitted.

She seemed to accept that without pursuing the subject further.

"So have you figured out what you're going to do with me yet?" she asked.

"For the foreseeable future I get to keep you," he smiled. "No real choice. You wouldn't be safe anywhere else I can think of for the time being."

Christine looked miserable. Her bruises darkened and she didn't just feel worse as she had told him. She looked worse, too. He noticed that the mirror in the bathroom had been flipped over so that she didn't have to see herself while she used the truck's bathroom.

"I think I better give you something for the pain again."

"I don't like drugs, but I don't think I have much choice either."

Mark fed her some food and gave her another round of painkillers. It wasn't long and she drifted back to sleep. He noticed the tension in her face leaving as her body relaxed. Visions of Nicole dead on their living room couch once again flashed through his mind. Where could he send her on a long-term basis? He felt he couldn't afford to have her along for the ride distracting him. He liked her. He couldn't deny it. He was stuck with her and deep down he knew he would bond with her the longer they were together. Right now he had no choice.

Mark needed to get some sleep and it wasn't going to happen here in the parking lot. He decided he would drive north until he came to a motel. He figured that he would find one in Orangeville. This way he could get the rest he needed and also be well on his way to a place where he and Christine could lay low for a while. She could heal and regain her strength. His damn ankle could also heal and he could figure his next move. He had felt he was so close to finding and dealing with Rodrigues but he had to let it go for now. He had to be patient.

Brenda sat at the reception desk looking over the beached whale like form of Zap lying on the floor for a long time. Erasing all the pictures of Christine out of the computer hadn't taken long. Ripping the surveillance camera tape out of the machine and crumpling it took a few minutes more. She called the owner, but only got the answering machine, where she left a message. The rest of the time she spent sitting, waiting not sure what to do. She was too scared to sleep. The scratch on her throat burned.

More than an hour later, Zap opened his eyes and just stared straight ahead for another five minutes without moving. That creeped her out. She had to fight the urge to scream. Then one of his hands moved a few times before he staggered to his feet. He held the desk to steady himself, looked around him without noticing her. At last his unfocused eyes found her and she saw a glimmer of recognition.

"Wha... happened?" he mumbled.

"You don't remember?" Brenda said not sure what to say.

Zap screwed his eyes up trying to remember what happened but couldn't quite focus.

"Some guy busted in here, knocked you on your ass and stuck you with a needle," Brenda recounted. "I tried to get the gun out of the drawer, but he took it away from me. He then went downstairs and came back carrying that new girl, Christine, all beat up, over his shoulder. He forced me to erase her pictures out of the computer and destroy the camera tape. Called himself "The Shadow". I thought you were dead. I tried calling the main office but only got the answering machine."

Zap just swayed there in front of her.

Cote's return to consciousness was less pleasant. He found himself lying on the cold basement floor with just his shirt on and Christine's blood and vomit gluing him there. It took several minutes before he could even try to get to his feet. He crawled to the wall where he pulled himself off of the filth of the floor. His hip hurt something fierce and he couldn't remember why. He still struggled to make sense of things, when Zap staggered into the room.

"What happened?" he asked the big man.

"Some guy calling himself "The Shadow" busted in here grabbed the girl you were with and left," explained Zap, not understanding himself.

Cote reached back through the cobwebs of his mind. He could remember the girl. He remembered slapping and punching her pretty face. He remembered kicking her in the belly and laughing while she retched. The name "The Shadow" seemed to mean something, too. He knew it wasn't good. This whole think reeked of disaster and the sooner he could think the better. He found his pants, but not his coat. Brenda stood outside in the hall waiting her mouth set in a firm line. She helped him ascend the stairs and then helped him get cleaned up. They all sat silent in the reception area recovering their senses.

It took them a good hour before they had recuperated enough to start taking any kind of action. At that point, Cote got on the phone and made a couple of phone calls. In no time at all a team of investigators were there looking for clues. They were Rodrigues' men, not the police. They didn't find much. Best thing they still had was the ragged surveillance tape, which they hoped would yield something useful

By the time they finished their work, Cote recovered and took charge. Even Zap did his bidding without hesitation. There wasn't much to find, though. They still had a couple of pictures of

Christine in her business outfit because they were still in Zap's email outbox as well as the surveillance tape. Not a single fingerprint or other clue left by The Shadow could be found.

A couple of questions nagged at Cote. Why here and why now? What led Rathman here and what did he hope to accomplish? Usually when he made a raid, he did it with the purpose of costing Rodrigues a lot of money or to try to lure someone out in the open. The intent boiled down to disruption and to try and get information. This attack didn't fit the usual pattern. It didn't appear planned out with a great deal of thought. It seemed to be more of an outburst of emotion.

It did occur to Cote that Rathman must know how he was connected to Rodrigues. This conclusion disturbed him. He always thought that Rathman didn't have that knowledge. If Rathman knew then Cote also knew that Rathman followed his movements with the hope of being led to Rodrigues himself. It could have already happened. Part of Cote relished the work ahead. Perhaps Rathman had made a mistake here that would lead them to him. Maybe an appeal to the public for information would lead them to something. With this much risky exposure maybe they could go on the offensive against their shadowy nemesis.

Chapter VIII

Good thing his truck had an automatic transmission, because his sore right ankle made operating the pedals an adventure. He stretched his right leg over to the passenger side of the truck and used his left foot for the gas and brake, an awkward but functional solution. He drove to Orangeville and found a quiet motel. Before going in to book a room, he went into the back of the truck to shave off his moustache and goatee. Too bad, he thought, because they kind of suited him. Behind the desk, he had a pair of crutches stored. This wasn't his first sprained ankle. He then made his way from the van to the motel office.

Inside, one of the owner's kids, a teenage boy about fourteen, waited to serve customers. He booked the room and passed Mark the key, but was so engrossed in a handheld computer game that Mark figured he hadn't even noticed the crutches.

By Mark's best estimate, Christine would sleep until after dark so he left her on the cot and went into the room alone. Before going to sleep, he put up the do not disturb sign and made a big stack of pillows to elevate his foot. Then he drifted off to sleep. He would be up again in about six hours. Mark never needed more than three or four hours of sleep a night. It gave him a tremendous advantage in life, but right now he had a sleep deficit that needed to be addressed.

The ankle wasn't any better when he awoke, but he felt alert. Christine still rested in the back of the van, when he returned. She would wake up soon. He blamed himself again for not looking at the note she passed him when they parted. He could've shipped her home at that point. She would have been safe and he could have gotten on with his business. Phillip Brock would be put on ice until this ended one way or the other. He knew his cover would without a doubt get discovered. Cote might be a monster and Rodrigues an old man but they weren't to be underestimated. He didn't know how close he'd gotten to Rodrigues' headquarters but part of him thought it had to be close. The closer he had gotten the more likely his cover was blown. Maybe the answers he looked for were right in front of him. Maybe he just hadn't put the pieces together the right way yet.

Christine began to stir. He went to get some food ready for her and by the time he brought the quick meal to her, she lay wide awake wincing with every movement. She looked at him hard for a few seconds.

"You look different," she said and then she looked like a light just went on in her mind. "Oh, no beard or moustache. Sorry I'm slow."

"I don't think you're slow," he answered. "When I was in college a buddy just shaved off his full beard and moustache. He was still wiping the shaving cream bits off his face, when one of the other guys looks at him and says, you look different without your glasses."

Christine started to laugh and then stopped wincing in pain. "No funny stories okay. It hurts too much."

"Sorry, didn't mean to do that to you. We have a couple choices to make right now and I want to ask you what you want to do. We're parked outside a motel right now. I rented a room and had myself a good sleep. I'm ready to go if you want to get out of here. If not, you can stay where you are or go in and sleep in a real bed and have access to a real bathroom."

"If we move on, where are we going?" she asked.

"We're heading for Wasaga Beach on Georgian Bay: Toronto's cottage playground. I have a cottage where we can stay while we heal and figure out what to do next."

"I want to go use the real bathroom in the motel and then I want to get out of here," she said.

With that, Mark rolled open the sliding door. There were only a few cars in the parking lot and night had fallen. Mark stood with his crutches and offered his arm to steady her as she got up and stepped out into the fresh night air.

"You're hurt," she said.

"Yep, stumbled on a curb carrying you and that great suitcase of yours. Aggravated an old basketball injury. C'mon let's get you to the room before someone sees you and thinks I'm some kind of wife beater."

They made their way to the door of the room and went inside. After the inside of Mark's truck, the room looked spacious and inviting. Part of Christine wanted to stay for a while but she shook it off. She wanted to get to where they were going and be done with the traveling for the time being. She gasped in horror when she saw her reflection in the bathroom mirror. She didn't realize she looked that bad.

"Have you got a painkiller that isn't going to render me unconscious?" she asked when they got to the van.

"I could give you regular codeine," he answered. "You'll be a little dopey and you'll still feel quite a bit of pain."

"Give me some then," she said. "I'm going to ride with you in the front. It's real dark and no one is going to be able to see me anyway."

"Are you sure? It'll be a lot more comfortable lying on the cot in the back," he advised. She gave him a determined look. "Suit yourself," he said with a shrug.

He rummaged around in his first aid kit and pulled out a bottle of codeine tablets and a jug of spring water and offered her a couple. After she washed them down with some water, he then helped her get into the passenger seat of the van.

"If you change your mind I can always pull over and you can get in the back again," he said.

Once he was certain she was comfortable, he made his way around the front of the truck and got into the driver's seat. Christine looked at him with raised eyebrows, when he stretched his right leg over to her side and positioned is left foot on the brake.

He grinned at her. "This is how we got this far. In the back you wouldn't have known. Now you're going to be scared all the way there."

She made no comment and pretended it didn't bother her at all. She didn't relax though until they manoeuvred without any problems out of the parking lot and onto the highway.

"So who are we going to be once we get there," she asked, once they were well on their way.

"Clarence and Joanne Vandenberg," he said without hesitation. "I take care of a group of cottages up there. I don't have to be up there much because if something goes wrong they leave a message and I call a repairman to solve the problem. I sometimes go up there to winterize them in the fall and on rare occasion I will actually go there for a little rest and relaxation. By the way, we've been married for about three years. Don't worry. Nobody there has ever met you and they barely know me."

She sat absorbing that for a few moments. The codeine started to do its work. The pain wasn't as bad and she felt pretty mellow.

"I got a question for you, now," said Mark. "How did you find out my real name?"

"You were featured on America's Most Wanted the other day. I recognized you from the pictures they showed but not just that. I remember the official version of your story from when it happened. My Aunt Yvette was your mother-in-law. Nicole and I are cousins."

Mark's jaw fell open.

Christine continued, "You probably remember that when you all moved to Quebec part of the family shunned you guys. My Mom looked down on her sister Yvette for marrying and staying with that two-bit criminal Nick Crowder. She painted you and Nicole with the same brush. That's the reason we've never met. When Nicole died the way she did it proved to Mom her point. I spent something like six months listening to her warn me about getting mixed up with a guy like Mark Rathman every time I went on a date."

"If only she could see you now..." Mark added.

"She'd faint in shock," Christine stated trying hard not to laugh. "Here I am not just hanging out with someone like Mark Rathman, I'm with the real Mark Rathman and I've gotten mixed up with real criminals to boot."

Mark bit his tongue knowing that if he said anything funny they would both laugh and Christine would suffer for it.

"Aunt Yvette and Grandpa both think you were framed and someone else murdered Nicole. Grandpa told us that both he and Aunt Yvette see a car at the cemetery regularly with people in it just waiting and looking. They think these people are there in case you show up. My Mom just scoffs at them."

"So what do you think?" Mark asked.

"You lied to me about it on the train but what else could you do? You still wear your wedding band and when I asked you about it I could see real pain in your eyes. If you had murdered her, I think you would have thrown out the ring. I also don't think you would have rescued me vigilante style. You would have let them beat me up, rape me and turn me into a hooker," Christine said.

Mark's face went hard. "They weren't going to turn you into a hooker."

Christine looked confused. "They weren't?"

"Ever heard of a snuff movie?" Mark said his face still grim.

"No. What's that?" not sure she wanted to hear the answer.

"It's sick stuff. I read a couple stories on line and couldn't understand how that could turn anyone on. Basically it's a sex movie where one or both of the participants are killed at the end. I stumbled upon this guy's last victim. You weren't going to come out of that room alive."

It took a while for the horror of it to sink in and she sat silent for a short time shaken.

"Is he the one who killed Nicole?" she asked.

"Actually no. This is the respected police officer who engineered the crime scene to implicate me so his real boss's nephew would stay out of hot water," he answered. "If he had done it I would've already killed him. Can't destroy the whole monster if I just cut off one of its arms, though. This world would definitely be a better place without him."

"That guy beating me up was a police officer?" Christine said in surprise.

"Guess you just figured out why we aren't leaving this in the hands of the authorities," Mark answered.

They drove in silence for a while after that before Christine spoke again, "I never met my cousin. What was she like?"

"If you had dark hair, you and Nicole could have passed yourselves off as twins," Mark began. "The way you talk and carry yourself reminds me a lot of her, as well. She was so full of life. I really miss her."

"She looked that much like me?"

"Family resemblance is hard to miss. I figure that's what triggered my nightmare on the train. Same petite build. Some of Nicole's clothes are still on our sailboat where we're going. I'll bet they'll fit you perfectly."

"So she was skinny and scrawny like me," Christine said.

"Skinny and scrawny? Who's been feeding you that line of bullshit?" Mark asked. "Nicole was beautiful and so are you."

"Zap called me that and worse," Christine answered with some shame. It occurred to her how stupid that sounded.

Mark laughed and added with gentle sarcasm, "Glad to hear you're quoting an authority on beauty."

"I did get a look at myself in the mirror back there at the motel. I'm ugly and that's the truth," Christine countered.

"That'll all heal. You'll see. It won't even take as long as you think," Mark said.

Christine decided not to push her luck on this line of conversation. Zap managed to hurt her self-confidence and hearing Mark tell her he thought her beautiful with obvious honesty made her spirits rise. The physical pain seemed more bearable and she contented herself to be riding beside him in the truck and talking with him. She didn't know what his intentions were long-term but she would do her best to make it difficult for him to move on without her. Mark, for his part, resigned himself to her presence. He wasn't sure having Christine around would be in either of their best interests. For the time being he had no choice though.

"One thing I never understood. What did my aunt ever see in Nick Crowder?"

"Nick wasn't such a bad guy."

"Are you kidding?"

"No, really he wasn't such a bad guy."

"But he spent most of his life in jail. Last time was for rape. Wasn't it?"

Mark eyed her for a moment, mulling his response. "His victim waited a month before reporting the rape. She kept working at the same restaurant with Nick and your aunt the whole time. During that month, this woman watched the two of them fall in love and get married. She was from a wealthy family and hired one of the best most aggressive lawyers in the state. He couldn't afford a lawyer himself. He already had a very long list of convictions for petty crimes under his belt. That lawyer tore him to shreds on the stand. Only person there to support him was your aunt. Sound like a fair trial to you?" "Doesn't sound like he got a fair shake there but why would she get involved with someone like him in the first place?"

"Nick was trying to fly right when he met your aunt. Had a legit job and was by all accounts doing good work. They worked together. She was the only one who treated him like a human being. He would have done anything for her. LA is a tough town for a Canadian girl. He took care of her."

"You're being vague."

"There are specifics you won't pry out of me."

"You do your own investigation or something?"

"Didn't have to. A few days before Nick died he asked me to have a private talk with him. Man to man. Confessed everything to me. Felt like a priest by the time he was done."

"...and you believe it all."

"No reason not to. He knew he was dying. If Nicole hadn't donated blood, he would have already been dead."

"She donated blood? I thought she despised him."

"For most of her life she did. She had a big heart though. Had a capacity to forgive that I sometimes wish I had. She was the only match they could find. The doctors said it might give him another week. For that week, they were a real family. Meant the world to all of them."

Mark let Christine mull that over for the next few silent miles.

"Do you know if he wrote her from prison?"

"Nick was illiterate. Couldn't write his own name."

Mark stared out in front of the van into the distance very quiet for a few more minutes. "Last thing he said to me was to take care of his daughter... Didn't do such a good job of that."

They arrived in Wasaga Beach in the early morning hours. The season wasn't yet in full swing yet so the town slept. They pulled off the main road just west of the town onto a small side street and pulled into the driveway of an older well-maintained cottage. Mark cut the motor and went into the back of the van for a couple minutes, returning with a box. It contained several big key rings full of keys. All of them were numbered. He selected two keys and removed them from one of the large rings and put them on a smaller ring.

"Let's go in," he said to Christine.

He manoeuvred himself around the front of the van with his crutches. Christine already opened her door by the time he got there and he stood so that he could support her. She winced a few times getting out but had no difficulty walking with him to the side door of the cottage. He unlocked the door and they entered. It smelled and felt empty. Christine had to wait a few minutes by herself in the dark, while Mark found the main power switch and turn on the electricity. When the lights came on they revealed the interior of a cozy three-bedroom cottage. Besides the layer of dust, it looked clean and neat. It was furnished with older furniture. The beds looked comfortable. Mark hobbled around turning on the heat and water and checked to make sure everything worked.

"So, do the Vandenbergs sleep in the same bed together?" Christine asked.

"Nope," Mark replied, "Clarence snores like a freight train and hogs the blankets. Joanne got sick of it years ago. Have you decided which room you want to sleep in?"

Christine just smiled at him because laughing would have hurt too much. She chose a bed in one of the smaller rooms leaving the master bedroom to Mark. Mark accepted that with a little surprise, but didn't say anything. She made her way over to her room and sat down on the edge of the bed realizing how tired the drive up had made her. She lay down and fell asleep on top of the blankets, before Mark returned with her belongings. He got a blanket and covered her up so that she wouldn't get cold.

Mark decided to catch a few winks before sun up, as well. The cottage warmed with the heaters working. Not a whole lot else he could do before daylight anyway. Groceries would be bought in the morning because they were almost out of food. After that he'd get a chance to get that ankle elevated and give it some of the rest it needed. He would get the satellite TV, Internet and the telephone hooked back up within the next couple of days. Cooped up in this place with Christine and nothing to do would not be a good thing.

Chapter IX

A few days later in Toronto, Marv Lindsay was summoned to Serge Cote's office for a private meeting. Lindsay disliked the man intensely from the day he arrived, but couldn't think of a valid reason why outside of gut instinct. He just got the impression that Cote would talk to you like your best friend while he pushed a knife deeper and deeper into your back without you knowing it. Cote's image as the perfect police officer and his well-established accomplished career didn't make him any more likeable. That had a lot to do with him being in charge and Lindsay still taking orders from people like him. Lindsay preferred his job this way. He still worked on the streets in tune with the pulse of the city.

Lindsay surveyed the small office as a hobbled Cote beckoned him inside. It contained a small desk with a computer, minimal decoration except a spot on the side displaying Cote's various awards from over the years. He motioned for Lindsay to sit with his usual good charm, and then winced as he descended into his own chair.

As he looked as his superior, a realization struck him like a sledgehammer and he struggled not to let it show. Cote visited Zap's whorehouse house just before Mark Rathman had spoiled someone's party. Lindsay hadn't recognized him at the time. That could only mean one thing. The man who assaulted the girl Mark rescued sat in front of him. Now he had a real reason to hate the bastard. This also made Cote Rodrigues' dirty cop. Completely above suspicious at this point, Lindsay ruefully admired him and, at the same time, felt total revulsion.

"Recognize this man?" Serge asked tossing, a photo of Mark into Lindsay's hands.

"Sure do," Lindsay answered, "Mark Rathman, wanted for murdering his wife in Montreal a little more than a year and a half ago. His father was a cop in the Niagara area. Worked with him for years. He died in a car accident right about the time Mark graduated from high school."

"If I understand correctly, you and your wife were quite close to the Rathmans," Serge continued.

"Sam and I were good friends. Spent a lot of time with his family. Saw a lot of Mark growing up," Lindsay replied.

"I've heard rumours that suggest he's in town. You keep your ear close to the ground. Have you heard anything?" Cote asked, looking Lindsay in the eye.

Lindsay feigned mild surprise, "Nothing from my sources."

"He slipped out of my fingers twice in Montreal and I'll be damned if he does it again," Cote said, still staring Lindsay down. "I need to know what you think and what you know." Cote paused a moment before continuing. "Do you think he's guilty?"

Lindsay thought some before deciding it would be best to be honest, "Bluntly, no."

"Then why doesn't he turn himself in and let us get to the bottom of it?" Cote demanded.

"Don't know. I wish he would," Lindsay lied. "A lot of us who knew him and his Dad, would put in a lot of work to help him clear his name, if he's innocent."

"Why? All the evidence I've seen says he's guilty," Cote continued.

"Because it's out of character. Mark was a great kid. His Dad had to be the best undercover cop I've ever met," Lindsay responded returning Cote's glare.

"Sam Rathman, the underworld knew him as The Shadow. You know his son uses that name as his calling card now."

"I've heard but there was never any proof that Sam and The Shadow were the same person," Lindsay returned.

"C'mon that's bullshit Lindsay. You were his partner and friend, how could you not be sure if he was The Shadow or not!" Cote's anger flared.

Lindsay stood his ground, "You don't know the state of morale in the Niagara Regional Police at that time. Sam played his cards really close to his chest. I suspected but he never told me one way or the other."

"Stop giving me crap about some kind of morale problem. What difference does that make?" countered a still angry Cote.

"Look it up. We just locked up Sergeant Gardiner. Used to send him to all the schools as our main public relations figure for the kids. Big beefy guy, model cop, ass raped some young boy. Nobody knows how many other kids he molested over the years. Wear your uniform out in public after something like that. Then the chief gets himself in hot water for looking after his friends. He should have just quietly resigned before things really got bad. We took public heat for that for more than a decade before they forced him out. Dogged with corruption rumours all the time makes it hard to do your job after a while. Especially when there is truth to some of it. After Sam died, I moved to Toronto so I could still do the work I love and hold my head up high."

"Okay, I'm sorry I never knew all that," Cote said. "Didn't mean to piss you off. I just don't take it well when someone makes me look foolish."

"Foolish...?"

"Like I said. Rathman slipped through my fingers twice in Montreal. First time I just plain underestimated him. When his wife was murdered, he sent us on a wild goose chase by buying a bus ticket with his credit card bound for Quebec City and then went toward Ottawa on his bicycle. Bought him about a day and a half. Based on some reliable sighting of him leaving Montreal we cast out our net figuring he could make about a hundred miles per day. Never heard of marathon cycling before. Turns out he rode non-stop all the way to Ottawa before getting on another bus under a false name. He ran more than a hundred miles ahead of our most generous estimates. We didn't figure it out for more than a year. He rode the bus past Sudbury to Espanola where they remembered him because he reassembled his bicycle right in the bus station and then disappeared. Trail cooled off by that time. We don't have a clue where he went from there."

"He's incredibly athletic. We could have told you that," Lindsay remarked hoping to keep Cote talking.

"Second time happened right after the Rejean Rodrigues murder. We had him cornered in the Montreal subway and he embarrassed us. He mingled with the crowd at the Beri-Uquam station and just vanished. We had cops at every exit and three more searching the crowd for more than an hour. It took almost a week of going over surveillance camera footage to figure out how he managed to just disappear. He put on a hat and sunglasses, pulled out his harmonica and joined busker Doleful Dave in the hall who plays blues guitar there every day. They played until long after we gave up and left. One of the boys even remembers them playing three blind mice. Gave the security camera a friendly wave when he finally left."

"Ooo, rubbed your noses in it," Lindsay commented hiding his own amusement. Sounded like the kind of stunt he and Sam would have pulled in their younger days.

"We questioned the guitar player but he knew nothing. Rathman tossed a fifty in his guitar case when he got there and another one when he left."

"So why do you think he's in Toronto now?" asked Lindsay.

"Just rumours from some of my old contacts back in Montreal. If he's in town, I'd really like to catch him before bad stuff involving him starts happening here. To do that, I'm looking for any tidbit of information about him or his dad that you can give me."

"Like I said before I only suspected Sam of being The Shadow. He never shared his methods with me. I know his main target was the drug traffic crossing the Canada/US border. He infiltrated several gangs and set up a lot of successful drug raids."

117

"I assume he passed on all his knowledge to his son, Mark," Cote added.

"That's a safe assumption. We all wanted Mark to be a cop like his Dad. I think, until his parents died, that's what he wanted, too. He then elected to study in California and get away from everything. I haven't seen him since."

"Any signs of violent behaviour from him?" Cote probed.

"Only once. He flipped out at the end of a basketball game with rival Notre Dame of Welland. He had martial arts training since early childhood. He was good, too. Had the makings of a champion, but didn't really like to fight. He's a rare combination of size, speed and strength in case you hadn't noticed during your own investigations. Uses it mainly to stay in shape and improve his focus in other sports. The other team goaded him all game long punching him and crap like that when the refs weren't looking. Took down everyone stupid enough to get close to him. He got a three game suspension for that."

"Maybe that's what happened between him and his wife," Cote added. "That sounds like a dangerous temper."

"I doubt it, but maybe you're right. Only person who really knows is Mark himself," Lindsay conceded. "I haven't seen him since he left for college, so that's pretty much all I can tell you."

"I know you like to haunt the back streets of Toronto, Marv," Cote said shifting the subject. "Since I asked you to stop wasting your time chasing after Zapparoli. What project are you working on now?"

Lindsay anticipated this question. Cote's subtlety impressed him. He gave a lot of thought over the last few days wondering when this would come up and who would be doing the asking.

"I've been haunting the harbour area trying to shake out some information on the McKenzie brothers. They're always up to no good," he answered with a little grin.

"Good, good," Cote nodded absently.

Lindsay thought it all funny. If staking out Zap could be considered a waste of time it paled compared with wasting time and effort on the McKenzie brothers. The fact that Cote was pleased at least on the surface just meant that Cote wanted him clear of the action. Rodrigues was smart enough not to have anything to do with a couple of idiots like John and Terry McKenzie.

"Well just thought I'd touch bases with you," Cote finally said clearly indicating the meeting was over. "I'll let you get back to your work."

Lindsay left, pleased with himself. This meeting gave him a whole lot more information than Cote got. He decided he would steer clear of this as he promised Mark with the exception that he would gather information from within the police force on all this and make his own file at home. Maybe he could find out a few things chasing after this from a different angle. He'd have to be careful though. Give any kind of hint that he was doing any kind of snooping around on this one would get him in a whole lot of hot water. This crime ring should not be taken lightly. It had cost poor Sam his life and now Sam's son lived as a fugitive from everyone because of it.

Chapter X

Mark got out of bed at about four in the morning and worked through a limited version of his customary morning exercises. Abbreviated because of the limitations his ankle put on his routine. He got his foot elevated all the way up on the dining room table and went to work on his lap top computer. He got a surprise, when at around six thirty in the morning Christine came, out of her room and sat down next to him.

"You're up bright and early," he commented.

"Not really," she answered. "This is sleeping in for me. I'm used to getting up an hour earlier than this. Am I bothering you?"

"No, just finished up some writing," he answered. "Phillip Brock is the writer and he won't be able to submit anything to his publisher for a while. Will be just holding it back for now."

"I won't stop you from writing," she said worried she was bothering him. "I can go back to my room if you want."

"You aren't my prisoner," he said, looking at her, a little concerned. "I know we have to hide out but I want to make this as pleasant as possible. Phil is on ice for the time being. I'm pretty sure my very poorly planned rescue probably blew that cover."

"I really screwed up your life didn't I?" she stated looking glum.

"I'm the one who screwed up," he replied. "Had I been smart enough to listen to that little voice in the back of my head, I would have looked at the note you gave me before you got in the taxi and I would stopped you from even going into that place. No injuries, no blown cover, no having to hide with you, just would have sent you home to the eastern townships."

"You still must think I'm pretty stupid for getting into all this," she said.

"Don't think that way," he replied. "You haven't struck me as being stupid, a little naive maybe but not stupid. You need another round of painkillers?"

"Yeah, I hurt really bad, still."

"I'll get the codeine seeing as you look like you don't want to sleep the day away," he said still looking at her concerned. She acted a little more morose than he would have liked.

He left her sitting there for a few minutes, while he hobbled over to get the painkillers for her. At the same time, he picked up a tube of antibiotic cream. When he got back he gave her a couple of tablets, which she took, trying hard not to let him see how much she hurt.

"Now hold still while I apply some of the ointment to the gash over your eye."

She held herself still while he applied the ointment to her injury with a Q-tip.

Making a poor attempt at small talk he asked, "Did he kick you in the face to make that gash?"

She started to lose her composure, "No he punched and slapped me... Said I wasn't doing it right... He made me..."

Mark realized his mistake and shushed her, "I'm sorry Christine. I shouldn't have asked. You don't have to tell me. I hate him plenty already."

Tears streamed down Christine's cheeks and Mark took her into his arms and held her being careful not to squeeze her and cause her pain. She cried and sobbed for almost twenty minutes. He remembered holding Nicole like this and the memory almost overwhelmed him. He missed her so much. He felt to cry along with Christine. When she regained her composure and stopped crying, she snuggled against his chest for a few moments and then backed off.

"I'm making you think of Nicole aren't I?" she more stated than asked. "I'm sorry I know I'm not the only one here with emotions."

Mark didn't know what to say. Her perceptiveness even under extreme stress surprised him. He liked her and couldn't help but feel for her some, but he missed Nicole and anything that reminded him of her gave him a hollow pain right in the middle of his chest.

"You hungry for breakfast?" he asked, when he found his voice.

"A little," she answered through red-rimmed eyes.

"Good. I hope you aren't fussy. I haven't had a chance to go to the store and pick up supplies," he said. "I have a box of Cheerios and some milk left in the truck."

"It'll do," she smiled.

Mark went and got the cereal and milk and was soon back. A blast of cool lake air came in the door with him. They ate neither of them quite sure what to talk about.

After the meal, Mark said, "I better go to the store and get some groceries before lunch."

"I'm not complaining about the food,"

"Even if you were, I still have to buy food. There isn't anything in the cottage here and what we just ate emptied the little fridge in the truck. Have a hankering for anything specific. Just say the word."

"I'm okay. What do you want me to do while you're gone?" she asked.

"You don't have to do anything," he said. "Dr. Rathman says you are supposed to be resting and healing. I don't really want you doing much else. I'll try to get the satellite TV working before I go so you won't be bored."

"Have you ever actually watched day time television?" she asked.

"No, usually don't have time. Why?"

"TV isn't a cure for boredom," she answered, "but I won't complain. Promise I'm not going to be more of a problem for you than I already am."

He managed to get the satellite TV up and running before he left, anyhow. The customer serviceperson told him it could be anywhere between fifteen minutes and two hours before the programming would come through. Turned out it only took about five minutes.

Although he felt bad knowing he left her with nothing to do. Getting out of the cottage proved therapeutic. Christine reminded him of how much he hurt when Nicole died. It made the pain all fresh again. Christine seemed like a sweetheart but he needed to get away from her for a little while. It wasn't just the memory of Nicole part of him yearned for that kind of relationship again and his attraction to Christine even bruised up like that reached out to him. He felt disloyal. He just needed a chance to get his head together. Sort out his feelings. There wasn't room in his life for all this.

Wasaga Beach is strung out along the waterfront on Georgian Bay and Foodland, the nearest grocery story, was clear across town. From downtown Wasaga Beach, if you could call it that, Mark's cottage sat almost a third of the way to Collingwood nestled in among the trees between the main road and Georgian Bay. It turned out to be a bit of a drive. Picking up a week's worth of groceries for two people ended up bringing back other memories. It felt so domestic. He often picked up the groceries when Nicole was alive. The whole day resonated in a way that made his heartache.

When he got back he found Christine moving about in pain, dusting the whole cottage. The dishes were already all washed and put away

"Hey you're supposed to be resting!"

"I'm sorry," Christine answered with a sheepish look on her face. "I just got sick of the TV and couldn't help myself. I thought if I cleaned up some, it wouldn't smell dusty and empty in here."

Mark looked at her and just shook his head. She needed to be resting and instead she worked at housework that quite frankly didn't need to be done at least not right now. To him she looked about ready to fall over. He admired her spunk but this was a little ridiculous.

"What am I going to do with you? I want you to have a seat in my big recliner over there," he said, "and take it easy. I'm going to make us some lunch. After we eat I expect you to take a nap if I have to drug you to make it happen. When you get back up I'm going to have to teach you how to watch TV. I want you to recover not kill yourself. Now go sit down before you fall down."

"I'm sorry," she said, "I just feel so useless. It's so boring here all by myself."

Mark managed to convince her to take a nap after lunch. Her efforts around the cottage tired her out. He wondered how on earth he would keep her entertained, while the both of them healed. He decided that while she slept he would watch the television with his ankle elevated. He got an ice pack for it and sat on the floor with his foot up on the couch. He flipped through the channels until he got to one of the sports networks and watched a basketball game. He got to watch the most of the game before Christine got back out of bed

"Hi. Whatcha watching?" she asked as she slumped down on the couch next to Mark's foot.

"Basketball game," Mark replied eying her strained face with some concern. "Looks to me like your painkillers are worn off again. I can get you some more."

"I can wait till the game ends," she said.

"Judging by the look of you, I'd say you're trying to tough it out so as not to bother me," Mark observed.

"Well I don't want you to feel put upon," she answered.

"You're way too apologetic right now. I'm your doctor and nurse and I'm going to get you what you need." Mark got to his feet hobbled over to the medicine cabinet and got the Tylenol threes for her. "Hopefully in a couple days you won't need this stuff anymore. It'll go faster if you leave off the housework until then."

The basketball game was almost over by the time the painkillers started to kick in and take the strained look away from Christine's face.

"You used to play basketball in college, didn't you?" Christine asked trying to make conversation.

"Played four years for Cal-State in California," Mark answered. "Saying I played though is being a bit generous. Spent most of my time riding the pine."

"I find it hard to imagine you being less than awesome," she remarked. "You have to be the fittest person I've ever met."

Mark pointed to his raised ankle, "In basketball circles I have what they call white man's disease. Constantly banged up ankles and knees. By the time I graduated I wore so many support bandages they called me the Mummy."

She laughed and Mark knew she was picturing him bandaged up head to foot. Her facial expression said it all.

"Laughing starting to hurt less?"

"Still hurts. I'm starting not to care as much."

"I've cracked a rib before and it hurts for a long time. You'll probably still feel it some six weeks from now."

"I've kind of resigned myself to it."

"Just don't try to be too tough. It won't help."

They continued to watch the game and he explained the action to her as it progressed on the basketball court on the TV screen. He knew she wasn't really interested in the game though. She seemed to find him far more entertaining than the TV. He just wondered how long it would take him to be talked out or for her to get bored of it all. Only way to get her to rest for the time being seemed to be to talk to her.

Chapter XI

Zap had never been invited to meet with the head honcho before, which made him rather nervous. Cote who came and picked him up assured him that he wasn't in any trouble over the mess that this Shadow character created. The whole fiasco created the need for this meeting though. Cote dug up quite a lot of new information on their adversary based on his investigation. From all he heard the Shadow had been a real pain in the ass for quite some time and this bit of interference in business just made the list of attacks longer.

Cote filled him in on the background on their way to Brampton. The original Shadow had been a thorn in Rodrigues' side when he ran drugs across the border in the Niagara Falls area. This guy cost Rodrigues lots of money but he couldn't figure out his identity. Through a contact in the police department, he learned Sam Rathman had something to do with the case. He learned that Sam and the family would be traveling to his son's high school graduation. Rodrigues sensed the Shadow moving in for the kill and, out of desperation, he arranged for an accident. They were run off the road right into a bridge abutment on the freeway. Normally there were barriers set up to lessen the impact but a deliberate accident earlier that day removed most of the barrier. Everyone in the car died and that ended the reign of the Shadow. Rodrigues' wild guess had paid off. No more Sam Rathman meant no more Shadow, at least that is, until about a year and a half ago. Mark ran off to college not wanting to have anything to do with police work.

Rodrigues' stupid nephew was the reason Mark Rathman started haunting them as the Shadow. Rejean tried to collect a drug debt a relative owed from Rathman and got turned down in rather humiliating fashion. Rejean couldn't let sleeping dogs lie. He went out to try and get some payback. Cote warned him to back off, but Rejean went ahead anyway. He of course took the payback too far. Instead of just roughing up Rathman's wife, he got carried away and killed her. Mark escaped and became just as much trouble to Rodrigues' empire as his father Sam had been.

Zap understood the humiliating fashion part real well. He'd never lost a fight in his life before he met Rathman. He beat up a few guys who thought they knew martial arts before so his defeat came as an unwelcome surprise. He wouldn't even have known what had happened except for recovered surveillance video of the whole embarrassing incident.

They pulled into the parking lot of a very tall apartment building and continued right on into the parking garage. They got out and walked over to the elevator. Cote punched a code into the telephone keypad and then they waited.

"Special code," Cote commented with a shrug. "This sometimes takes a while. The elevator won't come down for us until there is no one in it. When it gets here it will take us to our destination without making any stops."

Zap nodded in response. He expected high security. As Cote predicted the elevator took quite a bit longer than expected. When the empty elevator finally arrived they wasted no time getting inside. Zap noticed that the floor indicator wasn't changing, when the elevator began to move. It stayed on the P for parking. By the way the elevator moved, he thought they were going up, but he wasn't sure.

When they got to the top, heavily armed guards greeted them. Cote surrendered his police pistol and they passed a hand held metal detector all over him before moving on to Zap. They took his gun as well as his knife before he was given the ok to proceed down the hall with Cote. The hall looked like the hallway on the floor of any other apartment building he had been in. The only real difference was the guards by the elevator and another pair of guards at a doorway further up the hall, where it looked like they were headed.

When they got there, they were patted down before being allowed to enter.

They entered an ordinary looking boardroom. The only face sitting around the large walnut boardroom table that he recognized besides Cote was Morrison who collected the profits from his business once a month. He assumed that the scrawny wizened guy at the head of the table had to be Francois Rodrigues himself. He looked frail with tanned, deeply lined skin. Zap was kind of surprised because he had always thought of Rodrigues as being a more imposing figure. This guy looked like he could kick the bucket any moment. His shrewd dark eyes sized up everyone as they came into the room and those dangerous eyes commanded respect. By the time all the last stragglers were checked and seated, the room was full.

This was Serge Cote's show today. As he rose to speak he looked pleased with himself but also troubled. He had a small remote control in his hand, with it he dimmed the lights and turned on the projector on the table facing the wall.

"A couple of you gentleman have no idea why you are at this meeting," Cote began. "By the time we're done I am hoping that it will be clear. Everyone important is here plus everyone that we know has had some kind of contact with the

Shadow whether they knew it or not. Not to worry anyone in trouble is already dead. "

With that pronouncement, an audible sigh of relief came from a couple of confused faces at the table.

"First of all, for those of you who don't already know, Mark Rathman, alias the Shadow, struck Mr. Zapparoli's establishment two weeks ago, disabled Mr. Zapparoli and myself before grabbing one of the girls and running off with her. Absolutely not his style but my preliminary investigation is complete and I've managed to make some sense out of it. Compared to past incidents we got ourselves a wealth of information."

The projector threw the image of Mark Rathman's license photo from several years before on the wall. A couple of gasps came from the audience.

"This of course is Mr. Rathman, alias the Shadow," Cote continued. "He did not leave a lot at the scene but we did recover parts of the surveillance tape that he attempted to have destroyed before he left. By the timing of his attack, I assume he had knowledge of my appointment time, which could only mean that he was able to intercept messages between Mr. Zapparoli and myself. We could find no evidence of a wiretap on either end. I assume the worst - that he got his information from my end of the communication. I decided to check out other surveillance tapes from other buildings to see if I could find an individual matching his description snooping around. Sure enough and he got a lot closer than I thought. Take a look at this driver's license."

Cote pressed a button on his control and a second driver's license image joined the first one on the wall.

"This is Phillip Brock, pizza deliveryman. Some of you have met him, because he has been delivering pizzas to this and the surrounding buildings for nearly the past four months. He rented a basement apartment not very far from here. He visited every single floor of this building except this one for obvious reasons. I don't think he is aware of its existence because on his most recent visit it still looked to me like he was searching. I'm not sure though. This guy is good. By the time I'm done here, I hope the rest of you understand how good because I don't want him to come back to bite us.

"From the pictures you see right now you can see that these are photos of the same person. I was able to speak to Rocco Moretti his employer at the pizza place but could not get any useful information that I didn't already know. I could not meet this Brock person because right after the dust up with Zap and I he disappeared. We broke into his apartment. Clean as a whistle. Not so much as a fingerprint. Evidently he was smart enough to understand that he might have compromised his cover. I know more but we'll get back to him as we go through the rest of the information I have."

Cote again pressed the button on his control and the pictures on the wall were exchanged for some shots of Christine.

"This is the girl Rathman grabbed and ran off with. Her name is Christine Jette – cute little bitch. She had been recruited by an associate of Zap's in Granby, Quebec at a bar. Just broke up with her boyfriend - wanted to get away from the area - small town girl who wanted to see a little more of the world. She was invited to Toronto to work for Zap and was given tickets for the bus from Granby to Montreal and for the train from Montreal to Toronto. I wondered how she connected to Rathman because it didn't make any sense. We interviewed her parents and her ex-boyfriend. Her parents of course are quite upset about her disappearance and, as far as the police in the area are concerned, her ex-boyfriend is the number one suspect. If we had a body we could pin it on the idiot, too.

"She is a cousin of Rathman's dead wife, but they had never met. Rift in the family or something and it all checked out. No apparent connection between these two people until I checked the passenger list for the train she came to Toronto on. Guess who else was on that train? Phillip Brock. Had some business in Montreal for a few days. I did have a couple of passengers from the train interviewed and it turns out that the two of them sat together on the train. Apparently they hit it off and left together. I can only make assumptions from there. They parted before she arrived at Zap's establishment.

"Somehow he intercepted communications between Zap and myself and came to rescue his girlfriend. Normally the Shadow is a lot more careful when he hits a target. I think he acted on the spur of the moment. Usually his attacks are very carefully planned and we get nothing useful. This time, however, I learned a lot. Miss Jette was injured before she was grabbed but we have searched every hospital and clinic in the area for her. No sign of her anywhere. My assumption is that these two are together and are laying low somewhere under assumed identities."

Cote proceeded to flip through all the pictures that they had on both Mark and Christine.

"If any of you spot anyone that somewhat resembles either of these two I want a report. We will check out every sighting. I don't expect to catch them this way but you never know we might get lucky."

Cote switched the picture on the screen to a video showing various martial artists trying to kick in a door. "We had the pleasure of having the Canadian karate champion in town for a competition and invited him and some of his friends for a little challenge. As you can see, the door took a beating but wasn't easy for them to break through." He switched back to the surveillance tape from Zap's business. They watched as Mark first took Zap out with ease and then skipped forward to see him blast through a similar door with one mighty kick. "We knew that the Shadow had martial arts training but this really surprised us. We were able to calculate the force needed to do the damage he did with one kick to that door. There are only a handful of people on the planet able to generate anywhere near that kind of power. In short, I don't want anyone to try and take him on one on one.

"He has a unique knife fighting style. In one hand he will carry a k-bar Israeli commando knife. In the other, he holds a double end Daga. Never seen anyone fight like that. Just when you think you can handle him he will switch hands. He prefers to disable opponents. The damage he does is usually proportional to his opponent's skill. The better you are the more likely you will suffer a severe injury. We know of several arms and knees he's broken. Rejean's death clearly shows he's not afraid to kill someone if the need arises or he's pissed off. Even our security personnel here have been told not to face him one on one. He will kick your ass and we will not be any further ahead. Incidentally our Canadian champion saw that clip and recognized Mr. Rathman. They faced off in high school. Rathman won easily."

With that, Cote turned off the projector and turned the lights back up. He wasn't finished yet though.

"Gentlemen, we have cracked one of the identities the Shadow uses. It tells us a lot. I have never in my entire career as an investigator seen such a carefully crafted undercover persona. Usually these kinds of identities go back a number of years and then there is a blank where there are no more records. Phillip Brock's record literally goes back his full lifetime without serious gaps. I thought at first Rathman had replaced an actual person. There are signs that the record was tampered with, though, especially near the very beginning when Phillip or Mark would have been a toddler. My conclusion is that at least this cover identity was created for Mark by the original Shadow his father Sam and maintained by Mark. Phillip Brock wrote fiction for teenagers and worked odd jobs here and there like delivering pizzas. He was making a decent living as a completely separate identity. Good covers are hard to crack. Without a lucky break on our part, we would have never figured this one out.

Francois Rodrigues finally spoke himself, "So what are we going to do about him?"

Cote responded without hesitation, "He was checking out the buildings here trying to find our headquarters. He stopped searching with the pizza delivery boy cover because he ran into a complication in female form. He wasn't done snooping around here. He'll be back. The question is, who will he be when he gets back? He knows that Phillip Brock is no longer a safe cover. How many other covers did he and his father develop and maintain? It takes a lot of work to build and maintain covers like that. There can't be that many of them. Our advantage is that we know he is going to come back here. The man is six foot five and over two hundred pounds. You can only dress something like that up so many different ways. We have to tighten security here. Anyone coming into these buildings that could remotely be him has to be identified and thoroughly checked out. We're going to have to dig really deep on a lot of people. Also, anyone already living in the building that could potentially be him in disguise has to be watched. The goal is to uncover his identity before he knows we are on to him. Then he can be caught and eliminated."

Rodrigues nodded, "Sound like we're looking for a needle in a haystack."

"True enough but at least we have something to work with," replied Cote. "That's a whole lot more than we've had for more than a year now."

"Find him and kill him," was all Rodrigues said.

"Before we finish, gentlemen, I want you people to keep an eye out for Marv Lindsay. He's hanging around the docks, annoying the McKenzie brothers. Don't do anything to help those idiots get themselves into trouble. The longer he's chasing them the less time he spends getting in our way. I know he worked with Sam Rathman before but I don't think he's involved. Just tell me if he starts staking out anything else. I'm sure you all know he's easy to spot. Grey coat, grey hat, and older blue Ford Taurus sedan you'll probably notice from about three blocks away. If you forget about him and do something stupid, he'll make you pay. Keep alert for him. I don't trust him to do what he's told. Now it's back to business."

The meeting broke up and the men got up and made their way over to the elevator. Cote clapped one of the men on the back good naturedly, "Porter, feel real bad, don't you."

"Hey, I had no idea," answered the man.

"I know he comes off like a really nice young man. Rocco over at the pizza place was telling me that he was the best deliveryman he had. Customers really liked the guy. Don't worry I've got your back. You've seen him and heard his voice. We can use all the eyes and ears we can get on this one," Cote assured him.

The man visibly relaxed with that. He worked as a computer technician for Rodrigues. He lived in the building and had ordered pizzas for his family often. Gave generous tips, as well. Never suspected a thing. It came as an enormous relief that he still had his job and his life.

As they went down the elevator together, Zap said, "So, I came along because I'm another set of those eyes and ears."

"Yeah that and from what I've seen of you you're a good man to have around in this kind of business," answered Cote.

"You know I didn't get much of a look at him," Zap added.

"No, but you know better than anyone what the girl looks like. That's important, too," Cote reminded him. "This girlfriend already helped uncover a lot of information for us. I don't think he's finished with her. I think she's given us another small advantage we didn't have before."

Zap smiled, as he understood

Chapter XII

Early in the morning, Mark once again perused a file on his laptop showing several of the high-rise apartment buildings Rodrigues owned in the Toronto area. He'd lost count of how many times he'd stared at these plans over the last few months and didn't feel any closer to solving the riddle of where Rodrigues' elusive headquarters were. He didn't get a good night's rest and felt more than a little frustrated. At about a quarter to six in the morning Christine came out of her room and settled in beside him.

"Had another nightmare like you had on the train, didn't you?" she stated rather than asked.

"Did I wake you up?" he asked.

"No, I was on my way back from the bathroom when you started thrashing around and making weird sounds," she answered. "Same dream you had on the train when we met?"

Mark debated with himself a little before answering. He wasn't sure how much he wanted to tell her. On the other hand, rescuing her drew her into his own private prison and now they were kind of cellmates. He fought this war alone for so long he found it hard not to talk and reveal a great deal about himself. Her obvious interest didn't help. Finally he answered, "Yes, it was the same dream. It haunts me now and then."

She sat for a while and then asked, "Did you want to talk about it?"

"Not really," he answered. "It isn't very pleasant."

"Sometimes it helps to talk it over with somebody," she said with a shrug.

"Talked about it a few times with Nicole way back when," he muttered looking away.

"Oh, I'm sorry," Christine, said puzzled now. "I thought she was in it."

"She is now," he gave Christine a quick glance realizing what she thought. "You're in it sometimes too. You almost ended up like the rest of them. I'd rather not see that become reality. "

She sat staring at him for a while until he took notice and returned her gaze. "I'm going to harass you until you tell me about it now," she said. "You really don't expect me not to want to know."

Mark pushed the laptop further on to the table and let out a long breath as he leaned back. His elevated foot rested on the corner of the table because of his ankle. "Kind of set myself up there didn't I?" He didn't wait for an answer. "My parents and younger brother Michael were traveling to my high school graduation on the QEW which is the main highway in the Niagara area, when they were run off the road by another vehicle. They crashed into a bridge abutment. Normally there are barriers that help avoid really serious crashes but there had been another accident and there wasn't much left of the barriers. My father and mother were killed instantly while my brother hung on a little longer. He died in the ambulance on the way to the hospital.

"My dad worked as a special investigator with the Niagara Regional Police. At the time, he was investigating a cross border drug smuggling operation run by someone named Francois Rodrigues. The other car involved in the accident disappeared along with the truth but it is common knowledge on the street that this wasn't an accident. I stored the information my dad collected on Rodrigues' gang at a hunt camp my family owns on Manitoulin Island. The property deed is in one of my Dad's many pseudonyms. I never looked at it until after Nicole died.

"My family have been policemen for generations. Everyone expected me to follow in my father's footsteps and if not for that accident I probably would have. I couldn't bring myself to face it, so I decided to pursue my artistic side and went to university stateside. I ran away from everything. I told everyone that I wanted to test my basketball skills against the best, but really it was just my excuse to get away from everything.

"I started having the dreams in college. I dream I'm in a cemetery and visit a morgue where all my family is lying shrouded on tables. I get to look at all their dead faces. Then I get forced onto an empty table by Rodrigues where they shoot me in the head. Francois Rodrigues' nephew Rejean murdered Nicole. When she died the dreams got worse and included her and the twin baby boys developing inside of her. On the train, you invaded my nightmare. You were alive but I got to watch helplessly as Rodrigues and Cote finished you off. That woke me up. By the way, that whorehouse where you were supposed to begin your new job is owned by Rodrigues, as well. He started out just smuggling drugs. He branched out into other shady enterprises a long time ago. Told you it wasn't pleasant."

"Does my being with you bring them on?" Christine whispered.

"Naw, I'd have them, anyway. I should have known better than to take public transportation and try to sleep," he answered. "Lucky I didn't make more of a public scene than I did."

"I'm glad you took the train. Would you have come to my rescue had you not met me already?" she asked.

"Probably would have," he answered. "I don't know if I could have had that on my conscious. On the other hand, the timing of events might have been different. Might not have stumbled across the message in time to do anything about it. Might have found your mutilated corpse. One of those what if scenarios you don't want to spend too much time thinking about."

They were silent for a while. Mark noticed that the swelling on Christine's face had gone down for the most part. Lots of discoloration around her eye still but that would soon begin to fade, as well.

"If you hadn't fallen into their trap eventually it would have been someone else," Mark said

"So you're saying I was just lucky," she replied a trace of a smile playing on her lips.

"If you want to call it lucky," he responded. "You getting hungry for some breakfast?"

"You want me to whip something up?" she asked.

"Ribs all healed up?"

"No. They still hurt just as bad as before."

"Then, no. You're still supposed to be resting. Besides I've been sitting here looking cross-eyed at those files for hours and am still drawing a blank. I have to get up and move a bit. I'm in the mood for a stack of pancakes. How about you?"

"I could go for that," she answered.

"While I'm doing that, look at those files. They are plans for eleven high-rise apartment buildings owned by Rodrigues. I'm convinced his headquarters are in one of them. I've delivered a couple hundred pizzas to all of them and have visited virtually every floor and can't find any sign of it. The one on the screen right now is my prime suspect. If you can give me one clue that I've missed, I'll take you out to a restaurant of your choosing as soon as you're healed up enough to show yourself in public without raising questions. After my cooking, you'll probably appreciate it."

Mark made his way over to the corner of the room where the stove and other kitchen equipment were, while Christine stared at the computer screen. She didn't make sense of anything before Mark returned with a couple of plates of pancakes some butter and a bottle of maple syrup.

"Judging by your facial expression, you are getting nowhere," he grinned. "Don't feel bad I've been staring at those plans like that for about three months now."

"Sorry I'm not much help. Only thing I know about those tall apartment buildings is that some of them don't have a thirteenth floor because people are superstitious," she responded. "Any other ways I could earn a dinner date? Why are you looking at me funny?"

"Write down the numbers one to eleven on that sheet of paper I have on the table there,"

Mark answered. "Good now look at each plan and write down the number of stories in the building and then the first two digits of the apartment numbers on the top floor."

Mark watched as Christine carefully wrote the numbers in columns on the sheet of paper. It took a little while for her to collect all the information from the files. Mark could see right away that she had hit on the key to this riddle that had been baffling him for so long.

"Notice anything different about one of the buildings?" he asked when she finished.

"Yes the columns match on your prime suspect but all the others are off by one," she answered.

"Which means?"

"Which means that building has a thirteenth floor," she continued.

"And that extra floor is where Rodrigues' headquarters are," Mark finished. "Right under my nose all this time. I guess your next job is to research local restaurants and figure out where to go to collect on this."

"We better eat our breakfast first," she glowed. "It's starting to get cold."

Serge Cote supervised the installation of a few more surveillance cameras. He wasn't stupid enough to think that they would be missed by the Shadow. The only way they were going to get anything on him with these was if, by some stroke of luck, they could get him to react without planning his moves again. Wish that somehow they could get their hands back on the girl. That had to be the biggest chink in his armour. Maybe they'd catch a lucky break. It would take a lot of patience.

In the meantime, they had to make Rodrigues' headquarters as secure as possible. From the security tapes he got the impression that Mark didn't know where they were through his pizza boy probing. That might be true but even if it was, it wasn't impossible that he might figure it out without performing more physical scouting trips. What kind of disguise would he use to try and get back in? Would he go that route? Scaling the building seemed an improbable option because there were no open balconies just enclosed solariums. He had no doubt that Mark could scale the building without too much trouble it just seemed unlikely that he would come in that way. Still he didn't want to rule out the possibility. He worried he might have missed some weakness that would allow Mark to bypass all their security and get in the same.

Something else bothered Cote. He felt certain that Mark knew all about him, and almost certain that the security breach that brought Mark to Christine's rescue had to be on his end. The Shadow had no other useful reason to be watching Zap's whorehouse. Besides that, he seemed to know what Cote would be doing with the girl. He knew it wasn't going to be just a roll in the hay with a whore. Cote felt more than a little insecure. He couldn't shake the feeling of eyes watching him. He also deduced that the Shadow had been onto him from the start. The implications were not pleasant. If Rodrigues went down, he would go down, too. The Shadow wouldn't walk away and leave him in peace. Not after the part he played in covering for Rejean and not for the beating he laid on his new girlfriend.

He remembered when Rejean died almost a year ago. The Shadow stripped the door handles off the inside of Rejean's car while he partied with his buddies in a bar, doused the interior of the car with gasoline before fetching Rejean, forcing him into the car and torching the works. Not a pretty way to go. Kind of gave the bastard a pre-taste of hell. Cote could see the same sort of thing happening to him. In fact, he'd already experienced one nightmare along those lines. He had to find the Shadow before he found them or he had to force the battle to be on their terms.

The false alarms were nerve wracking. They'd already investigated a few people hanging around the building that bore some resemblance to a disguised Mark Rathman. They even checked someone out that looked a bit like the girl but they were all dead ends. He knew they would be, too. If he were the Shadow, he would lay low for a little while before probing the defences again. He would be back though. The question was when and how?

Chapter XIII

"Feeling a lot better I see," Mark remarked a couple days later. Christine stopped taking the painkillers and she moved around without much pain. The swelling had almost disappeared and the bruising began to fade. Mark's ankle improved, as well. He walked with just a bit of a hobble. The purple below the inside ankle bone started to fade. He knew after a full week he could resume normal activities and training. Might be more than a month before it would be back to full strength, though.

The two of them also slipped into a routine. Mark would get up real early, do his abbreviated conditioning workout, then shower and shave. By the time Christine awoke he sat well established at the dining room table with the laptop working out the logistics of penetrating Rodrigues' lair. Once Christine had freshened up and gotten dressed she would join him and they would talk some before eating breakfast. The domestic routine gnawed at Mark some. It felt comfortable and he didn't want it to.

"Where'd you get that sweatshirt?" Mark asked.

Christine glanced down at the blue top she wore with the words Wasaga Beach splashed across the front. "I remembered you telling me there might be clothes on the sailboat in the backyard that might fit me. While you went to the Laundromat yesterday I checked it out. I only took a few items I thought would be useful and I snapped the tarp covering the cabin back in place. You aren't mad at me are you?"

"No... Just a lot of memories in that boat. My dad built it with a little bit of help from the rest of the family. The name Pretty Fang was my idea."

"There are a couple photo albums stored in there, too. I'm sorry I couldn't help myself. I had to look."

"Really. What was in them?"

"The older one was filled with pictures of you and your family when you were a teenager; mostly vacation pictures. The other one had pictures of you and Nicole on some kind of boating trip... You were right, we do look like sisters."

Mark smiled and shook his head, "Now I know where those missing albums disappeared to. I haven't been aboard that boat since we stored it after our vacation that year." Mark paused for a moment, and then said, "You're going to be a real handful when you're back to full strength, aren't you?"

Christine decided to change the subject. "What do you plan to do once you've put Rodrigues and his gang out of business?"

"I plan to travel to Montreal and visit Nicole's grave," he answered after a brief pause.

Mark looked over at her and he could see the wheels turning in her mind. She scrutinized him, trying to gauge his thoughts. At times, she seemed to understand him far better than he felt comfortable with

"I know how important that is to you," she said. "Have you given any thought as to what you plan to do with yourself after that?"

"I don't have any plans after that," he said with some force. He regretted saying the moment it came out and looked away from her gaze. She appeared concerned but didn't pursue the subject. It bothered him. He felt as if she read his mind. He obsessed about the subject for a while after Nicole's murder. What remained for him after that? His family were all in their graves: His parents, his younger brother and his wife. His unborn twin boys never took a breath. He planned to kill himself when he got there. That way he didn't have to think about making plans for a future with no meaning. He wondered if he had the guts to go through with it. He wondered if Christine guessed at the meaning of his answer. He suspected she did. He could lie to just about anyone but he got the impression that she could read him like a book. They sat silent for a short period time while Mark pretended to be studying the plan of the building on the computer in front of him.

"Do you have any ideas for getting in there yet?" she asked still eying him.

"A few," he responded relieved at the change of subject. "When my ankle is healed I have to do a scouting trip to check to see if there have been any changes to the building security. I have to assume that they beefed things up since my last visit. I also have to assume that they know my alias Phillip Brock, as well. He gets to disappear for a while."

"You think coming to rescue me gave that away?"

"Without a doubt. They'll guess how I found out what was going to happen to you and they will check surveillance footage because of it. It shouldn't be too hard for them to figure out I've been delivering pizzas to their building for months. They'll also likely figure out the connection between us. Serge Cote is a pretty astute investigator I can't imagine him not figuring out that much."

"I just had an awful thought, Mark," Christine said wondering out loud. "What if they tried to lure you into another confrontation by getting another girl like me and ambushing you when you come to rescue her."

"That would be smart but there are a few reasons they won't try that," Mark answered. "First of all, they think we're going to lay low for a while and might not get the message. Secondly they might think we are in a serious relationship and I might not be interested in the bait. The real reason though is because Cote knows I won't go for the bait. I'll just kill him. He's intelligent, knows what he's doing but deep down he's also a coward."

"Would you really kill him?" she asked.

"Does that bother you?" he countered.

"You're serious. You really would kill him," she answered, "I have a hard time seeing that in you. Personally I'd rather see him behind bars for the rest of his life."

"I saw what he did to a girl in Montreal," Mark said. "It wasn't pretty. I really couldn't live with myself knowing that he would do that to someone else. I couldn't let him do that to you. Honestly I wanted to kill him then. He can't ever do it to anyone else if he's dead. As long as he's on the loose sooner or later there will be another victim. Putting him behind bars isn't as simple as it sounds. I don't understand a mind that can take a beautiful young woman like you, beat her to a pulp while raping her and finally finishing her off if the beating hasn't already killed her. We're far better off without people like that. That just has to be evil in its purest form."

"I just struggle with the idea that you're capable of killing someone Mark. It scares me," she answered.

"Scares me too, Christine," he said looking in her eyes. "I wish it didn't have to be that way."

Another long silence ensued between the two of them. Mark didn't feel so uncomfortable this time though. He was going to suggest he prepare breakfast, when Christine beat him to the punch.

"My turn to make breakfast," she announced.

Feeling much better, she bounced over to the kitchenette and went to work. It wasn't long before the smell of scrambled eggs wafted over to Mark and set his mouth watering. Christine's first time cooking for the two of them reminded him of the times he and Nicole vacationed in this same cottage a couple years ago. A pang of loneliness swept over him for a moment. He shook it off, when Christine arrived with a plate of food for him. He didn't want Christine to notice. The food impressed him but they ate in silence. Christine then insisted on cleaning up the dishes. When she finished she came back and looked at Mark with a sombre look in her eyes.

"Mark, there is something we need to talk about," she said continuing to eye him with that serious expression. "I'm healing up and soon will be able to carry on normal activities in public.

You'll soon be ready for action again, too. What I want to know is what you plan to do with me?"

"I haven't planned anything," he began. "I figured to cross that bridge when we got to it. I can think of a number of options but ultimately what you do is up to you. I'm not your jailer."

"What options are there?" she asked. "I can't go home and be myself because that would be walking right back into trouble not, just for me but for you too."

"Canada is a big place Christine," Mark answered. "There are lots of places we could send you to live until this is over. Clarence and Joanne Vandenburg could get legally separated and you could go just about anywhere safe in this country you want. The only places you would really have to steer clear of are southern Ontario around Toronto and your home area in Quebec. You don't have to make a decision right now though. Think about what you want to do."

"I already know what I want to do, but I doubt you'll agree to it," she said.

"Try me," he answered.

"Okay but don't laugh at me. I want to be able to live as myself as soon as possible. The only way that is going to happen is if you put Rodrigues, Cote and all those people out of business for good. I want to have a part to play in gaining my own freedom. I want to stay with you and work with you on this till it's over."

"I don't ask this to ridicule you, but how do you think you can help?" he asked.

"I can at least run errands for you and be a sounding board for your ideas. I said something that helped you find where Rodrigues' headquarters is... I'm sure we can think of other ways I can help as we go," she said, her gaze wavering.

"I hope you don't mind if I start with my objection," Mark said looking into her hopeful facial expression. "People close to me get killed. I've already seen you beaten to a pulp in real life and I've already seen you die twice in my nightmares. I really like you as a person and think of you as my friend. I don't want to see you die in real life. My inclination is to convince you to get shipped as far away from the action as possible. It really hurt me to see you suffer the pain you already experienced at the hands of that monster Cote. You're right though in that it's only fair that you get to play a part in gaining back your freedom and yes you have proved that you can be an asset. If that's your decision, I'm prepared to work with you."

"That's my decision," she said with conviction. "If not for you I'd already be dead, so the curse of being close to you is already working in reverse for me."

He laughed, "Maybe your curse is over powering mine."

"That's not funny," she answered laughing in spite herself.

Over the next few days, Mark and Christine began setting up a real office in the third bedroom. They stored the bedroom furniture in the shed out in the back yard and in its place they picked up some quality used office furniture and installed a full workstation with a proper PC, printer and scanner. Necessary office supplies were stored in the closet. The room already had an existing telephone jack but they had to run a cable from the living room for the Internet.

Christine rode in the truck with Mark on their errand runs. She didn't go into the stores, though. Her injuries were healing but it was still obvious that she'd been beaten up. They didn't want to have to deal with embarrassing questions or some do-gooder thinking Mark was a wife beater and ending up dealing with the police. They didn't need to attract that kind of attention. The activity was therapeutic for them both. They both suffered from cabin fever and they just needed to get away from the cottage.

"So you get to work as a Southern Ontario secretary after all," Mark teased.

"This office tells me that you're planning to go to Toronto and leave me here," she answered as if Mark was backing out of a promise

"I have to scout out our target first," he answered. "Your injuries are still obvious enough to present a problem. I don't want to keep you hidden in the truck the whole time. Besides you'll process the information I send you faster here than you ever could on the laptop crammed in the back of the truck. Another concern is where we will sleep. I can sleep in the back of the truck by myself and I'm sure you could as well but not at the same time."

"I want to play a more active role though," she complained.

"Let's go over my idea and see if there is a way to involve you more directly," he answered. "My idea is to bring my surveillance equipment in the truck this Saturday morning early. I plan to scout mainly on foot the entire grounds surrounding the building. I need to know everything about their exterior security. I need to know where they located all their cameras, infrared sensors and motion sensors. I also need to know if they have foot patrols and the schedules they follow. How many security people do I have to contend with and where are they stationed? I'm figuring to be there at least three nights before I head back here. That'll tell me if the weekend and weekday schedules are different. I can send you the pictures and information for further organization and analysis. Even if you just organize it all, it will save me a ton of time. We will communicate back and forth via cell phone and email. With all that information, I will come back and we will create our plan of attack."

"So you'll be gone for nearly three full days at the minimum," she noted with a frown. "If I come with you I have to be cooped up in the truck the whole time. You've left me nothing but really lousy options."

"If you come up with something better, I'm all ears," he answered. "I have to have this information. I know you understand that much. I know how to get the information that's needed without putting you or myself in danger. Saturday is the day after tomorrow. That still gives us lots of time to come up with potential improvements or even a different approach. This isn't set in stone until we put it in motion."

Christine did not push the issue any further but Mark could see she wasn't happy with the arrangement. He tried to soothe her displeasure by reminding her that she would have time to find a restaurant where he could pay up on the dinner he owed her. That seemed to mollify her somewhat although he got the impression that maybe she just humoured him on that count. She treated him coolly all day Friday before his departure. She didn't come up with other suggestions for this surveillance mission before it came time for him to head on out, though. Saturday morning before leaving she fussed over him until he left.

The lonely drive from Wasaga Beach to Brampton bothered him. Part of him wanted to get away from Christine. He had a job to do and determined to put her out of his mind. The loneliness he now felt had a new element that he wasn't ready to admit to. He had too much time to think while he drove down the road. The planning for this mission was pretty much all in place and there is only so much review one person can do before carrying out the plan. He found his mind drifting back to Christine over and over again.

Chapter XIV

Mark entered Brampton via highway ten, turned left on Queen Street and drove until he could access the parking lot for the Bramalea City Centre. He rolled into an empty parking spot where he had an unobstructed view of the apartment building on the other side of Dixie Road. He carefully counted the floors to confirm what he and Christine and had noticed from the building plans. While he did that, out of the corner of his eye, he noticed a man strolling through the parking lot with an electronic device in his hand.

Mark observed for a few moments as he drew closer. The man appeared to be noting license plate numbers. Mark restarted the truck and moved to another part of the lot, where he could continue to observe. After another ten minutes of observation, Mark spotted a woman doing the same thing and decided it might be safer to park further away and do his surveillance on foot.

He pulled back out of the parking lot and drove several blocks into a residential neighbourhood and parked on the side of the road. A quick check in call to Christine and then he walked back to the City Centre parking lot so he could continue his observations. His equipment consisted of just a few important items he could carry: a small high-resolution digital camera, a compact hunter's spotting scope, a notebook and pen.

The man taking license numbers finished a short time after his arrival. The woman continued on around to the south side. Mark noted the times in the notebook and looked for further signs of surveillance. Before crossing the road to take a closer look at his target, he noticed a couple out for a stroll. Most people who were on foot made their way over to the mall, but not this couple, they headed around the block for no apparent reason. Mark noted the time and their path in the notebook, as well. Just in case they weren't out for exercise.

Mark needed a better vantage point so when the couple cleared the area he crossed the road at the corner of Queen and Dixie. The ground sloping up to the building containing Rodrigues' lair offered a dense cover of scrub brush designed to prevent erosion. It also surrounded a mini mall complete with donut shop and convenience store sitting between the apartment building and Dixie road. As soon as he crossed the road, he disappeared into the bushes to continue his reconnaissance. He spent the rest of the afternoon working this area.

Mark took literally hundreds of pictures of the target building, he could see from there and the surrounding area. At the same time, he filled the notebook with notes. A great deal of data for Christine to process. Likely the bulk of this information would prove useless, but that didn't bother Mark at all.

He learned a great deal that afternoon. The man checking license plates turned out to be one member of a three-person team. Their surveillance seemed random and not thorough unless of course Mark missed another element. The mini mall featured tighter security. Nothing could come in without coming past the watchful eye of a surveillance camera. No donuts on this stake out. He identified several regular foot patrols: Two men and two women walking by at regular intervals. Mark got good pictures of everyone and noted the schedule they followed. None of these measures had been in place before rescuing Christine. Obviously Phillip Brock had been exposed. Mark didn't find anything much beyond his expectations.

Mark also took pictures of all the other buildings right nearby. Rodrigues owned four and he wanted to see what security changes had been made to those, as well. He would run through a complete analysis back at the cottage. He would be a whole lot more comfortable working there. Besides, he trusted Christine's abilities to organize the data he would send her.

With his initial daytime reconnaissance complete, just before dark he dodged the foot patrols and walked back to the van. He downloaded all the pictures into the laptop, used a scanner to upload all his notes and ate a quick supper. His earlier call to Christine served only as a check in. They didn't talk at that point. Right now thought, he had a bit of time to call and talk. He only needed to pass information to her and provide her with some direction, but he didn't need much of an excuse to chitchat. He already missed their conversations back at the cottage.

"Hi Christine, how was your day?" Mark asked.

"I'm lonely but I kept myself busy," she answered.

"You'll be busy now," he said. "Got over four hundred pictures for you to work with and I feel like I accomplished a lot. They've beefed up security since my last visit. Grabbing and running off with you really stirred them up."

"Just be careful," she said concerned by what he told her.

"I will," he assured her. "I'm going to sleep until about midnight and then I have more probing to do. I suspect they have a number of other "surprises" for me that I'll find tonight."

"You still planning to come back after four or five days?" she asked.

"No reason to think it will take longer at this point," he answered. "I'll come back then and try to analyze all the information I'm collecting. I'll also likely have to order some additional equipment. I'll know more in the morning."

"Do you think you're going to have a difficult time getting in?" she asked.

"I always find a way in. That's what I'm good at. That's also why they are so scared of me," he answered. "Don't worry too much. This mission is pretty much routine and I'm going to be steering clear of anything that appears to be potentially dangerous."

"All the same, I worry about you."

They chitchatted after that until they talked for thirty minutes. Neither one of them wanted to hang up at that point but they wanted to police their cell phone minutes and also stay on schedule. Christine knew that Mark needed sleep even if he slept only half as much as a normal person. They bid each other a reluctant goodnight. Christine retired to her bed missing Mark's presence more than ever. He went to sleep on the cot in the truck wishing that he could be back at the cottage.

Four hours later Mark's little alarm beeped in the truck and he returned to action. He did some quick stretches and pulled a case from under his worktable. It contained a small portable infrared scanner and some night vision equipment. After checking both to make sure they were in good working order, he went to work with the night vision equipment first. He planned to scan around the surrounding neighbourhood first, because others employing the same technology can easily see night vision equipment at night. On the bright side, it never ceased to amaze Mark how many people used these things. By checking out the neighbourhood, he could find other people using the same type of equipment and use their locations to mask his own observations. The infrared didn't have that drawback; it didn't create any telltale light show for other observers to see.

He meandered around some and quickly found what he looked for: Someone else awake and using night vision goggles. He turned off the equipment so as not to be observed. He then turned it back on at short intervals until the other user decided to turn in for the night. Mark then moved to a spot in front of that location and used his equipment to scan and take pictures of his target from a distance. He would be able to work with the pictures later. He also did a full infrared scan. He would do the same thing from as many angles as possible over the next three days.

By the time four days passed, Mark had taken an unbelievable number of pictures and mapped out the schedule of all the foot patrols. He managed to track all the human security people, get their license numbers and with whom they were connected. The work progressed at a steady crawl and he spent more time thinking about Christine than he felt he should.

His expectation that the security would be beefed up all round proved accurate. They moved additional night vision equipment to the premises. Additional motion sensors as well as several infrared scanners had also been installed. The infrared equipment would have seen his daylight visits but didn't have the range to cause Mark any immediate concern. Couldn't guarantee that Rodrigues wouldn't suspect something later when they had a chance to double-check their data. His own surveillance information piled up and he was grateful for whatever work Christine put into organizing it all. Mark sent it to her as he got with no attempt to organize anything in advance.

The drive back to Wasaga Beach seemed to take forever. He fought the urge to put the pedal down and attract some unwanted attention to himself by speeding. He arrived right about the time of his normal breakfast check in call. He gave the neighbourhood a careful going over first to make sure there wasn't anything out of the ordinary before he pulled into the driveway. Christine gave him a cool reception.

"You know we can't work together like this," she said

"Why not?" he answered with her looking steady at him straight in the eyes.

"Because I'm going to go completely nuts here with nothing to do but think of the danger you're in," she answered. "I want to really help you. This is my prison, too, you know."

"I want to keep you out of harm's way," he said. "We'll try to find more things for you to do," he said not wanting to argue.

"You will," she said with vehemence. "I want to show you something. Come on."

She led him to the backyard where he practiced throwing his throwing knives into a splintered plywood silhouette, when he had a little time to spare. The backyard offered complete solitude from the neighbours and Christine took advantage of it to get some fresh air.

"I found some of your throwing knives in the cottage and practiced a little while you were gone," she said. "Watch this. For inspiration I think of either that guy who beat me up or Zap."

With that introduction, she pulled out one of the throwing knifes and launched it at the target. It didn't quite fly the way she wanted it to though and it embedded itself right in the groin of the silhouette. She reddened and threw the second one, which struck the silhouette square in the chest. Mark walked up to the target to take a closer look at where they struck.

"You're not impressed are you?" she said still a little embarrassed by her first throw.

"You've been practicing for a couple days," he observed noting how far the knives penetrated the plywood. "I am impressed that you are throwing hard enough to actually hurt someone. Judging by that first throw you have a bit of a mean streak, too."

They both laughed before he added, "You throw like a girl though."

She pouted, "I am a girl or didn't you notice."

"That's not what I mean. I'm talking about your throwing motion. A lot of women use a push motion, when they throw something. It isn't efficient and it makes it difficult to generate a lot of power."

"How do I change it?"

Mark thought for a few moments. "Easy to say, not always easy to do. I'm not much of a coach but I can try to help. Watch how I throw first."

With that, Mark pulled the knife out of the target and proceeded to demonstrate proper throwing form. Christine watched with rapt attention.

"Now you try," he told her, after retrieving the knife.

As soon as she cocked her arm to make her throw, he said, "hold right there." He pulled her arm further back by the wrist and with his other hand he pulled her elbow forward a bit. "Now when you throw, move your whole arm forward, not just your hand with the knife. Look at your target. When you finish your throw you should be pointing where you want the knife to go. Now try it."

Christine launched the knife and it sailed over the target cleared the fence and landed in the neighbouring backyard. "Good, you just forgot to point at your target. Don't worry nobody is staying next door right now. I'll go get it when we're done." She practiced a few more throws with a great deal more success.

"Not that great, am I?" she said when they were done.

"Don't be hard on yourself I'm impressed that you even bothered to try," he said. "We can outfit you better later. The knives you're using are old dull ones. I'll show you where and how to hide them on your person, as well. I'm wearing a lot more of them than you think."

"Before I go in and start breakfast for you and you go retrieve your knife, I want to see you throw one really hard," Christine said.

Mark hesitated and then reached to the pouch between his shoulder blades and, in one lightning quick, fluid motion, threw with force at the target. Christine heard the knife hit the target but she only saw a hole in the target. It had gone right through. The knife stuck in the fence behind the target.

"Wow," Christine said eyes wide.

Mark's face reddened. "Just remember knife throwing is a useful skill but real combat with a knife is up close and personal."

"I want to learn."

"I'll teach you what I can as we have time. Just don't set your expectations too high and don't get cocky."

After breakfast Mark unloaded the truck. He also examined Christine's injuries. They were pretty much healed up. Just the red scar line just under the brow line over her eye showed. The ribs still gave her trouble but that was not something anyone could see.

"You know I think we could cover that with a little makeup and no one will notice it anymore," Mark observed.

"Almost ready to let me go out in public?" she asked, a little happier.

"I think you are. There's some makeup in one of the cupboards here somewhere. Let's see if we can make that bit of a scar disappear," he said leaving her by herself in the kitchen while he did a quick search. He came back with the makeup after a few minutes.

The cover up makeup did an excellent job. The thin red line disappeared almost completely. It wasn't even noticeable on close examination. Once that was done they delved into the material Mark spent four days gathering.

Mark wasn't the only one doing research. Back in Toronto Serge Cote brooded over the infrared security tapes from the week before. He did notice the heat source that scouted out the buildings that Rodrigues owned. At first blush, his team thought the image looked like that of a large dog. No animal would have picked those locations so well by accident, though.

He checked the area in person on foot. He found footprints but nothing very clear. Couldn't even identify the type or size of the person's shoes. He just felt certain of one thing - the Shadow had returned. The infrared image came up only during a four-day period of time. What did the Shadow learn? Did he find any flaws in the security that he could exploit?

Rather than change anything existing. Cote decided to double the number of foot patrols, using four more people. In theory the Shadow noted all the patrols that were there. Keeping those in place and leaving their schedules untouched might lead him not to notice the new patrols. He also assigned a few more people to range out further checking license plate numbers. He knew that wasn't enough but it made him feel like the initiative rested in his hands rather than just waiting for the Shadow to make his inevitable strike. The whole thing made him nervous though.

Chapter XV

Mark spent most of the rest of the day comparing before and after pictures of the apartment house. He made no effort to hide what he was doing from Christine. She sat next to him as he located new surveillance cameras, motion sensors, noting where the night vision equipment was being used and also noting the location of the infrared sensors.

"Those cameras cover just about everything by the look of it," she said noting the obvious.

"The infrared sensors, too," he nodded. "I don't doubt they picked me up sneaking about in the bushes. Probably didn't think much of it at first. Maybe thought I was a big stray dog. I'm betting they analyze this a little more closely and realize it was me."

"You don't seem terribly bothered," she said leaning against his shoulder.

"I can bypass all that," he answered. "I need to do a little inside reconnaissance but I'm pretty sure of what I'm up against. There is a soft spot in their security the question for me is whether they have it covered. The only way to find out is to go in and look."

"I'm scared for you," she said.

"Don't be," he smiled at her. "Even if they detect me they have to catch me first. My concern

179

with that is that it will put us right back at square one. Only I don't have a good second idea for how to get in there and take the whole organization down."

"You aren't going to tell me how you're going to get in are you?" she said pressing a little harder against his shoulder.

"You really want to know exactly what I'm doing, don't you?" he said.

"Of course," she answered all ears.

"I really can't get valuable input from you if you don't know what's going on now can I?" he continued.

He opened the plan for the building that was on his target. He enlarged it and focused in on the garbage collection area.

"The garbage truck visits this building every single day to haul away trash," he began. "A building like this produces a very large amount of trash. The truck comes in the middle of the afternoon. They unlock these big back doors and back in. There's a dumpster there under a garbage chute that runs from the top of the building to the bottom."

"You're going to get a job with the garbage disposal company and go in that way and have a look first and then access the hideout from the garbage chute," she filled in for him.

"Very good, you almost hit the nail on the head," he said. "The problem is that the guys who do this job will be thoroughly checked out by Rodrigues, people. Trust me, they are on the lookout for anyone remotely fitting my description. Besides that I need to be able to get in and stay in to do the work. They would probably notice if a garbage truck went in and came out missing a person."

"So how are you going to go in with the truck without being seen," she asked.

"I've traced out their route. I'm going to cling to the bottom of the truck with a backpack full of supplies so I can properly scout the place out. When we get there, I drop off and hide myself till they are gone. I need to see any interior surveillance equipment both in the room and in the shaft. I'm betting all is clear because they have the entrance covered well. When I'm done, I have to wait for my ride to come back the following day."

"That doesn't sound like any fun. Once you see that everything is clear, how are you going to get all that equipment that you've been ordering in there to be able to use it?" she asked.

"A little at a time," I can carry a backpack full every time I go in," he answered. "It's my only way in without being detected. I've learned to be very patient when doing something like this."

"Maybe too patient," Christine observed. "Does doing it this way leave you exposed for a very long time?"

"I can't think of any way to speed it up," he answered.

"You're forgetting you have a team mate," she said giving him a friendly shove. "You can't get in there through the front door because they are checking everyone who could be you. That probably narrows things down to just a few people because you are so much taller than average. On the other hand, I'm about the same size as not just a few women but also a large number of teenagers. I could dump packages for you down the garbage chute a couple times a day."

Mark was silent for a good while not wanting to admit it was a very good idea. It would speed up the operation substantially. The only part of it he didn't like was that it would mean Christine being right close to the danger.

"You know it's a good idea don't you?" she whispered.

"That doesn't mean I have to like it."

She decided not to push it further. It was time for her to be patient. Mark was in turmoil. He knew she was right and knew where this would lead. He wanted very much to find another way so that her help would not be needed. Trouble was that he'd been thinking this whole thing through for months and hadn't already come up with something better. He knew full well that he wasn't going to come with something better in the next couple days.

"Let's take a break," she said. "Now that I don't have to hide inside all the time I want to walk with you on the beach and watch the sun go down. Then we can sleep on this when we get back."

She gave his arm a gentle squeeze before getting up to go for the walk. They walked side by side far down the beach in silence. The sun went down as the waves gentled lapped at the beach. It was dark when they made their way back. The moon was full and bright.

Mark couldn't believe he was considering her modifications to the plan he had come up with. It was a great idea though and it would limit the time he would be exposed to danger by a lot. Not only would he be able to get his materials in faster he would be able to go in for longer periods at a time. He would be able to do in a week what was going to take him more than a month. He just questioned putting her in harm's way even if that's where she wanted to be.

In the morning Mark was working away at the laptop when Christine got up and joined him.

"Breakfast is ready for you on the stove if you're interested. Your toast just popped and the scrambled eggs are still hot," he said.

"Thanks," she said as she got a plate and helped herself. "What's the plan today?"

"I don't think we have a choice but to follow your suggestion," he said.

Christine was delighted but did her best not to show her enthusiasm. She just pulled her plate up closer and sat down next to Mark.

"It adds a little bit of work to our second reconnaissance trip," he added. "We have to plant a recorder somewhere near the front of the building so that we can get pictures of people who live there. From that, we can figure out how to dress you up to get in and bring me supplies."

"When are we going to do this?" she asked.

"Not sure," he answered. "We have to work out the details and get you costumed up for your role. We have some shopping to do for that. Anything else you can think of right now?"

"I made reservations for Saturday evening at the Georgian Inn Resort for supper," she said. "I hope that isn't a problem. You did tell me to plan something before you left so that you could pay up on that dinner you owe me."

"That won't create any problems. We can run this little mission Thursday and Friday. You get to plant the recorder first thing Thursday morning.

We'll retrieve the recorder after I go in and out with the garbage," he said, looking at her trying to gauge what she was thinking. "You get to spend a very boring day alone in the back of the van. You think you were going stir crazy here in the cottage. I'm hoping you decide you like it better here."

"I'll be careful. I know you don't want me in any danger. I do appreciate the trust you are putting in me," she answered.

They went over the plan for the day. Christine was to ride Nicole's old bike around the front of the building and fall off. She would pretend she broke something in her backpack and concealing what she was doing from the surveillance cameras plant the recorder in the flowerbed pointed at the front door of the building. Mark had enough memory in it to record everyone coming and going for a full two days. The quality didn't need to be good. They just needed to be able to dress her up well enough to pass her off as a couple of the people living in the building. The tricky part was going to be to retrieve the recorder without raising suspicions. She would dress up differently and come on foot to pick it up. It was going to be hard waiting in the van knowing Mark was in the building for twenty-four hours. They would do their usual cell phone check. No words, though; just clicking and popping sound patterns to let each other know if things were okay or not.

Mark wasn't sure he could get a signal, though, so if she didn't get anything she wasn't supposed to start worrying. That was easier said than done. They had to buy her some clothes that matched what the teens were wearing to make the look complete for the first part. The second outfit was intended to make her look like a young teenage boy. It didn't have to be that good. Surveillance camera resolution isn't impressive.

They had no difficulty getting Christine all dressed up for her part. She insisted on buying what she could at the used clothing and thrift stores not wanting to spend too much money. They only bought what they had to buy new. Then Mark surprised her by going to look at used cars to get her transportation.

"Mark where do you get the money to buy all this stuff?" she asked, just a little exasperated at his spending.

"Don't worry, I can afford it," he answered without explaining anything.

"Come on Mark. You've been living in hiding for a year. You can't possibly have made enough money delivering pizzas in Toronto to pay for everything."

"Actually a good pizza delivery man gets good tips but I make money all the time just sitting on my duff hanging out with you," he answered. "Phillip Brock makes money writing, which I'm sure you see me doing on the laptop all the time. That cover makes a decent living in his own right. Clarence and Joanne Vandenberg own and rent out twelve cottages here in Wasaga Beach and eleven more elsewhere. They bring in a very nice income from that every year. Those are just the covers you know about. Trust me, plunking a couple of grand down for a used compact car is really not a big deal for me. I may need you to be mobile while I'm using the van and doing this will come out cheaper than renting you a car."

"I'm just used to being a whole lot more careful with my money," she replied still a little uncomfortable with the expenditures.

"Don't go changing that. If you ever get married; whoever your husband is will appreciate that," he answered with a laugh. Mark noticed that she didn't find that line as funny as he did.

Chapter XVI

Wednesday evening they loaded up the truck and drove to Brampton. When they got there Christine slept on the cot and Mark did his best to catch a few winks on the floor. He did not sleep much or well, though. It wasn't just a comfort issue. Christine's proximity wasn't helping him either. No problem though once he was inside the building he would sleep more. He would have lots of time to waste in there because there was a limited amount he could do in there on this trip. He just went over the plan and tried not to think of what all could go wrong.

A nervous Christine succeeded in planting the recorder quite early in the morning. Mark had to clean up a scraped knee she got during the fake fall.

"You really didn't have to make it look that real," he teased.

"Don't underestimate how far I'm willing to go to make this work," she laughed. "Sorry I took so long. There was someone there and I had to wait for him to leave before I could do my little act."

"Better to be careful. We already backed off our drop point because of increased surveillance. I'm glad to see you keeping alert."

Mark put the truck in gear and headed for the garbage truck rendezvous point. His part of the operation was far more dangerous but he wasn't really nervous at all. He'd been living undercover for most of the last year and it was becoming second nature to him. This is what his life consisted of.

Christine got behind the wheel and started adjusting the seat more to her liking while Mark went into the back to make final preparations. He got out the side doors and walked around to her window. His hands were full of equipment.

"We're all ready. Time for you to take the truck and make yourself scarce until I get dropped off here tomorrow."

"I'll be here," she said with a worried look on her face. "Be careful in there."

Neither of them knew what to say at that point so they just parted. Christine drove off while Mark gave her a wave goodbye.

The drop point was just another apartment building on the same garbage route not owned by Rodrigues. When the garbage truck pulled up, he rolled out of his hiding place and attached himself to the frame members on the bottom of the vehicle. It wasn't a comfortable ride but he'd done this more often than he cared to remember. He detached himself as soon as he was inside the garbage area of his target. He timed his move, as the truck was getting ready to leave. He rolled out and hid himself beside the empty dumpster. As soon as the truck left and the big doors were locked he began looking around the room he was in. He was pleased at what he saw. No cameras, no motion sensors, no heat sensors, in fact, not a thing that could detect his presence. He looked at his cellphone and checked the signal strength. It had just enough. He hit his speed dial to contact Christine. When she picked up, he tapped the microphone twice and hung up. Now all he could do was wait. There was no sense going to check for surveillance equipment in the garbage chute until the wee hours of the morning otherwise he risked being taken out by someone's sack of garbage. It was going to be a very long boring wait. Didn't know who was going to suffer more for the next day him or Christine.

While he waited, he made himself comfortable and caught up on some of the much needed sleep missed the night before. He didn't go into action again until two in the morning. At that point, he checked the chute with his night vision goggles. No sign of any sensors there. Mark was in and able to go to work.

Climbing the garbage chute was very hard work especially carrying equipment with him. The sides were sheathed in sheet metal making it very slippery. Mark worked like a mountain climber climbing a rock chimney. He pressed his back against one side and his legs slowly walked up the other. He inched his way up, straining with the effort.

He stopped climbing at the fifteenth floor well above his target. He used a small hand drill to bore through the sheet metal and into the underlying concrete. It was painstaking, slow work since he was in an awkward position the whole time. Once he had his anchors in place, he attached his largest piece of cargo right there to the side of the shaft. It was an electric winch with a baffle to deflect garbage from battering it. There was a radio control device attached to it and a large battery pack. Mark took out a controller and tested it to make sure it worked. He then clipped himself to the cable and tested his weight checking the device to make sure it was secure. He had no desire to fall down the shaft. He then lowered himself with the device to the thirteenth floor and stopped. He stayed there and just listened for a while. There wasn't a sound. He didn't think he'd done anything to disturb the gang but he just wanted to be sure. He then lowered himself back down to the bottom got the cable wound up out of sight and started waiting for his ride to take him back out.

The long wait till morning garbage collection took an eternity to pass. He spent a lot of time wondering how Christine was handling herself living in the van. He was certain she was sick with worry. Maybe she would decide she didn't want to participate in the operation after all. He doubted that though. She had returned his double taps on the cellphone after every check in. So far everything was in order.

Right on time there was some clanking around with the lock to the garbage area and then the big double doors swung open. The garbage truck slowly backed in. It only went halfway in to the room but that was enough for them to manoeuvre the dumpsters so that they could be emptied. Mark calmly attached himself to the bottom again and off they drove until they were visiting another apartment building along the route that Rodrigues didn't own. Mark detached himself and rolled under cover. As soon as the garbage truck was gone Christine rolled up with the van and the two of them were reunited.

"You don't smell very fresh," said Christine wrinkling her nose. "You can clean up in the back as soon as we clear out of this place. We have to go, though. Those license plate checkers you pointed out when we first got here wander pretty far sometimes and we're in their range."

"I'm starved. The rations I took in there with me didn't hold me over very well," Mark said.

"Got you covered. I picked up a burger and fries for you before I picked you up. Not the best food but it'll fill you up. It's waiting for you in the back."

He grinned at her for a while. She was doing her best to prove to him that she was going to be an asset in their adventures. In his estimation, she was exceeding all expectations.

"How did you find the waiting?" he asked.

"I hated it," she said turning to him the strain showing clearly in her face. "It's necessary though and I will live with it. You've lived with this a lot longer than I have. I can be a real help and we will get through this faster and safer this way."

She pulled into a convenience store parking lot where they wouldn't attract any attention and parked the truck. Mark went into the back of the truck and got himself cleaned up. Christine was in the back with him before he was finished. As soon he was reasonably clean she nearly hugged him to death.

"Worried myself sick while you were in there," she said with obvious relief.

Then she let him eat. When he was done, they went over the map together and planned where Christine would get out and pick up the recorder and where he would meet her and pick her up again. She changed into her disguise. They managed to flatten her hair to the back of her neck and with the baseball cap she could pass for a teenage boy when she was done. They were ready early and had to do quite a bit of waiting before the time was right.

Mark let her off not far away from the target but it was a good bit of walking for Christine. She had to dawdle a little before making her approach because there were a couple people who were there and her disguise wasn't going to pass real close scrutiny. They left, though, and Christine walked up to the main entrance. Picked up the telephone and pretended to dial one of the apartments, pretended to talk to someone and then went outside and sat down on the edge of the flower bed where the camera was concealed. She pretended to be waiting for someone. Her seating position was no accident. She sat so that her body conceal her retrieval from the security camera. Shaking with nerves, she managed to fumble the camera safely into her backpack. As if on cue, a group of teenager ran out taking no notice of her. She ran along behind them pretending she was with them until she was a safe distance away. Then she walked until she got to the rendezvous point. Mark came along and picked her up right on schedule. Everything had gone almost exactly as planned.

They had supper in the truck on the way back to Wasaga Beach. They were both hungry. Tension has a way of burning up a lot of calories. When they arrived home Mark did his usual careful approach to the cottage before pulling in. It was a relief to be back.

Serge Cote stepped in the security room and paused. His hip no longer hurt and in that regard he was feeling much better.

"Miller! Anything of interest to report today?" he asked the nearest security guard. Miller lounged in his chair not bothering to even straighten up.

"Nah, nothing at all. We haven't seen a single repeat of those infrared images from about a week and a half ago. Not even a whiff of anything out of the ordinary since then."

"I don't like it," Cote noted wondering whether he should give Miller a dressing down for appearing lackadaisical. He thought better of it. "Carry on. Just stay alert."

"Fred and I got to watch some kid wipe her bike out on the step this morning," Miller added.

"Funny as hell. Scraped her knee and sat on the edge of the flowerbed crying. That's about all the excitement we get here."

Cote gave a curt nod and then left the room. He was not amused. Just over a week and absolutely nothing. He could sense The Shadow winning. Not a good feeling at all. He racked his brains trying to think of something he might have missed, something that might allow his nemesis to bypass security and get in.

Chapter XVII

Mark and Christine went over the pictures Saturday morning and found three good candidates for Christine to impersonate. Two were teenage girls living in the building and another was an older woman with grey hair that also lived there. The key was to match their clothing and general appearance. They wanted Christine to be able to walk by foot patrols without being detected. They also discovered that there were more foot patrols than there were before.

"Obviously someone saw my infrared images in the bushes on my initial scouting trip," Mark mused.

"Is that a problem?" Christine asked.

"Maybe, maybe not," he answered. "It did alert them to my presence. I imagine someone is starting to get nervous now that there are no other signs of me. It isn't impossible for someone to guess how I'm getting in. Just in my experience not very likely. Always have to be on my guard, though. I am prepared to fight my way out if I have to."

"Let's keep our fingers crossed that no one guesses how you're getting in," she said worried in spite of Mark's confidence.

Rounding up the needed clothes to imitate the two teen girls was going to be easy but expensive. The older woman's wardrobe would be a more difficult matter. For the time being, one set of clothes to match each person was going to have to do. They would work on getting more info later. Adding to the needed wardrobe would be Christine's job while Mark was busy working inside. It would keep her occupied instead of spending all her time worrying about what was happening with Mark. It was decided that she would be less conspicuous driving around town in the rental car so they would travel to Toronto in separate vehicles and meet at a prearranged rendezvous point.

"The only problem I can see is that I don't have a key for the front door of the building," Christine noted. "If I'm supposed to be someone living there I should have a key."

"Just a sec," Mark said getting up and heading out to the van. Christine was going to ask him where they were going to get a key but didn't have a chance. She made to follow him, but he was already on his way back before she got to the door.

"Here," he said presenting her with a key. "That's for the main entrance. I saw someone drop it while I was delivering pizzas and picked it up months ago. I tested it and it does open the front door."

Christine added it to her key ring and smiled at him.

"I thought for a minute there you had forgotten an important detail," she said.

"You just keep trying to find things I've missed," he said. "You just might think of something that'll save both our lives."

They worked hard until lunchtime. After a quick lunch, Christine insisted that they get ready for their evening out. With the excuse of changing her appearance a bit to help keep her from being recognized Christine drove over to the local hairdresser to get her hair done. Her real reason was because she wanted to look her best for Mark. She insisted that he get all dressed up, too, because the place they would be eating would be rather elegant compared to McDonald's.

As soon as she was out the door, Mark hopped into the shower to get himself washed up. He carefully shaved and then went about trying to find his dress clothes. He found them pressed and hung in the closet. That wasn't where he'd left them and he started to get the distinct impression that this was going to be a whole lot more than just a nice dinner at a restaurant.

Christine had put a great deal of thought and planning into the evening. When she returned from the hairdresser, she managed to sneak past him and into the bathroom without him having a chance to see what she'd had done to her hair. He figured she was planning to surprise him so he powered the laptop back up and did a little writing while he waited for her to reveal herself. It was a long wait. She finally came out wearing an elegant black strapless dress and black Greek sandal type shoes. She had gotten a perm and she looked positively radiant. When she walked in Mark was speechless.

"Do you like my outfit?" she asked, fearing he might not.

"Like it?" he said when he found his voice. "You look drop dead gorgeous."

"You really think so?" she said blushing just a little

"Let's put it this way," he smiled, "no one is going to notice me at the restaurant this evening."

"You almost ready to go?" she asked. "I'd like to go early and walk some, when we get there.

"I thought I was ready," he answered, "but I'm not sure I own anything that will make it look like I'm with you. I don't own a tuxedo. This plain suit and tie is the best I've got."

"Are you trying to tell me you don't want to go?" she said disappointment written all over her face."

"Christine, you look terrific," Mark said standing up and walking to her. I meant that as a compliment. I'm lousy at that sort of thing."

Mark offered her his arm and off they went out the door and to the truck. Mark drove toward the centre of Wasaga Beach assuming he was heading the right direction.

"I hope you know exactly where it is," he stated. "I never really went to many restaurants in the area."

"It's okay," she answered. "I got the address and made sure I could find it this afternoon when I went to get my hair done. I hope you like it, when we get there."

"You seem awfully nervous. Are you okay?" he asked.

"I'm fine," she said not looking at him.

"You're up to something," he observed with a grin. "I guess I'll find out sometime this evening won't I?"

She smiled but didn't answer him. He left it at that not wanting to upset her. She wanted the evening to be special. He hadn't anticipated that, but at this point he didn't mind. When they arrived, he went around and opened the door for her. They walked up and down the walkways and looked out over the lake, until it was time for their reservations. They made small talk the whole time, with Christine acting just a bit nervous right through. When they went in and presented themselves as Clarence and Joanne Vandenberg the hostess smiled and ushered them to a very private table in the corner with candles and all.

"I better tell you before someone says something and you get confused," Christine said still nervous. "I told them this was for our third wedding anniversary. You did say that Clarence and Joanne have been married for about three years."

"You didn't," Mark said giving her his best suspicious scowl.

"I did," she said. "You're not mad are you?"

"No, I'm not mad," he said. "I just was expecting to have a nice meal together beyond our collective culinary skills. Not a romantic evening for two."

"You aren't mad, but does it bother you?" Christine said still concerned. "I was afraid it might remind you of the past. I also wanted this to be a real date, not just a dinner pay off even if you aren't really interested in me. Kind of a girl thing... I want you to enjoy yourself with me this evening."

"Nicole was a tomboy, never wore a dress as long as I knew her, not even when we went to Las Vegas to get married," he said. "Never did anything like this. So don't worry about this reminding me of the past. You're charting new territory."

"You never went with her on a romantic dinner date?" she asked astonished.

"That's what I just said, we just weren't into that kind of stuff I guess," he said with a shrug.

"You prefer tomboys?" she asked with a hint of disappointment in her voice.

"No," he answered, "Just Nicole. Don't try to figure out what I like and especially don't try to be like Nicole. Just be Christine and let's enjoy ourselves. That's what you wanted in the first place isn't it?"

She nodded and smiled, relaxing a little bit. They ordered their food and chatted. They were given some complimentary wine, which Christine only sipped a couple times. She explained to Mark that if she drank up she would get tipsy very fast. He didn't say so but that did remind him of Nicole. She couldn't handle alcohol either and knew enough to only take a few sips to be polite, as well. Mark drank his own, but refused to have a second glass when they offered it. When they finished eating Christine started getting nervous again.

"Um, Mark there is a bar and dance floor upstairs," she began. "I was hoping to go up there with you and you would ask me to dance. I kind of prearranged the music with the deejay."

"I'm starting to think you're more dangerous for me than Rodrigues or Cote," he laughed.

Mark paid the bill and then allowed himself to be led upstairs to the bar and dance floor. There weren't very many people there. Christine went over to the deejay and chatted with him and came back smiling. A slow dance number started to play over the sound system.

"I figure I better do this right," Mark smiled back. "Would you like to dance, Christine?"

"I'd love to," she said matching his formal tone.

She took his arm and he led her to the middle of the dance floor. She snuggled against his chest as they swayed to the music, closing her eyes.

"You know this is very dangerous, what you're doing," he said to the top of her head. "You really should be wearing steel toed safety shoes for this."

"You're doing just fine," she answered with her cheek still pressed against his chest, eyes closed.

"For now," he said. "When the tempo goes up, that's when you'll be in trouble."

"The tempo isn't going to go up," she said maintaining her position. "Remember I picked the music."

"I underestimated how dangerous you really are," he said with a teasing tone. The he added more seriously, "When we get back to the cottage we're going to have a long talk. This might sound stupid but you really blindsided me with all this."

"You aren't mad at me are you?" she asked a little worried. She backed off and looked up at his face.

"I wish I could be," he answered. "That would really simplify things."

She studied his face for a bit before pressing her cheek back against his chest. Mark was silent for a bit not really knowing what to say.

"I want to run away with you," she said breaking the long silence.

"To where?"

"I don't know. Just somewhere away from everything. Somewhere we can forget about crooks and revenge."

"Tried that once," he answered. "Didn't work out very well."

"I know, but I can day dream."

They were silent again for a while.

After a few minutes he said, "You know you are slowly wiping the cover up make up over your eye on my shirt."

"You don't like to look at it?" she asked absently not changing her position.

"It doesn't bother me really," he answered. "Just makes me think sometimes how close I came to letting that monster Cote degrade and kill another innocent beautiful young woman."

"You know what I think when I look at it in the mirror?" she said backing off again to look him in the eye.

"No, what?" he said.

"I think of you coming and gently helping me to my feet, putting a coat on me. Then I remember seeing Cote and Zap lying unconscious as you carried me away from there. I remember you examining the injury every day and carefully putting antibiotic ointment on it with a Q-tip being careful not to cause me any pain. I remember you hobbling around without complaint because you sprained your ankle carrying me and my oversized suitcase," Then pressing her cheek back against his breastbone, she added, "Every time I see it in the mirror I look at it and feel like I belong to you."

Mark swallowed and stayed silent. His thoughts struggled together. He felt himself betraying Nicole with the feelings he couldn't deny he had for Christine. Part of him wanted to push her away and another part wanted to pull her closer. He did neither. He just kept slowly moving around the semi-deserted dance floor with her.

"Since Nicole's murder, have you ever conversed as friends with anyone besides me?" she asked him rather suddenly.

Mark hesitated, trying to think of another time he'd engaged in a conversation with anyone since then gave up and simply answered, "No."

"How have you kept from going completely crazy over the past year and a half?" she asked. "I could never handle the kind of isolation you've been through."

Mark didn't know what to say or even how to feel. He missed Nicole. She had been everything to him. His sole focus since then had been destroying the organization that took her away from him. Once accomplished it didn't seem like there would be anything left. Another long awkward silence enveloped them.

"Why are you surprised that I find you attractive?" she asked, shifting gears.

Mark shrugged, "I'm not exactly handsome."

"You're not ugly and you're in awesome physical condition," she said, making him blush just a little bit.

"I've never had to fight off the ladies," he responded, "except for a couple homely ones... and Nicole."

She giggled into his chest, "...and now me. You don't seem to be fighting, though."

He pulled her a little closer for a moment, and said with a laugh, "I'm losing."

She gave him a fierce hug and then backed off. "How long do you want to keep dancing with me?"

"We should probably cool it and head home soon," he said. "We have to put together a plan for taking down Rodrigues' gang starting tomorrow morning."

"One more song then and we'll head on to the truck," she agreed. "I managed to keep you prisoner a lot longer than I ever expected."

They thanked the bored deejay when it ended. Christine took Mark's arm and allowed herself to be led down the stairs and out into the parking lot toward the van. The temperature cooled off with a breeze coming in off the bay. Mark gave Christine his jacket because she got goose bumps on her bare shoulders as soon as they stepped out the door.

Mark guided the van through the darkness back to the cottage. They sat silent in the van. Mark couldn't think of anything to say and Christine didn't want to spoil the mood. The spell held until they re-entered the cottage. Mark mulled over what he would say to her and couldn't quite figure out how to begin. Christine waited a few moments before helping him out.

"You said something about us needing to have a long talk when we got back this evening," she said. "I'm ready to listen even if I'm kind of dreading what you're going to tell me."

That didn't help Mark at all. He chewed his lip and tried to look Christine in the eye.

"Just a sec," she added. Mark watched her retrieve a stool from the kitchen. She placed it on the floor in front of him and then climbed on it so they were looking eye to eye

"You're going to tell me that you don't want a relationship at all right now, but I knew that already," she said tearing up a little. "You like me as a friend, though, and don't want to hurt my feelings."

"I know this is going to sound stupid," he began, "but I didn't know before tonight that you had those kinds of feelings for me. You're right though. I don't want a relationship. At least I don't think I want one. The part that makes it difficult is that you are my friend and I am attracted to you both physically and intellectually. Worse, I trust you more than almost anyone else I know right now. I like you too much to just take advantage of your feelings for me."

"Part of me wants to be taken advantage of," she said wiping a tear from her cheek and smiling.

"Tomorrow we start planning how to take on fortress Rodrigues," he said. "Things are going to be plenty dangerous. Even without romantic distraction I could get myself killed. You do understand?"

"I understand," she said. "And I hope that you understand why I have to do this."

With that, she threw her arms around his neck and pressed her mouth to his. Mark didn't respond at first marvelling at the softness of her lips. She persisted finally encouraged when he began to kiss her back. He gave in for a few moments. His hands caressed her slender waist and back, pressing her lithe form harder to his chest. Her lips parts as she moulded herself to him, searching with her warm tongue lingering over his mouth. He traced her hip and then palmed her bottom for a second. He then broke their kiss and pushed her away some.

"Don't stop touching me, Mark."

"I can't..." he said, a tear on each cheek. He felt them burning there, but he refused to acknowledge them. He held himself stoically, seeing a hint of hurt in her eyes.

"It's like kissing Nicole again, isn't it?"

"No, it's different... It's real... I don't remember exactly how it felt..." Mark still held his jaw clenched tight. The tears streamed down his face now. "I don't remember exactly how it felt when we made love... Two weeks ago it was our anniversary and I didn't remember till the next day..."

She hugged him close again but didn't kiss him. "You're angry at yourself for being human."

They stood like that for quite a while before breaking away.

"Mark, if we take down Rodrigues and we both survive, take me with you to visit Nicole's grave."

"That is going to be a really personal moment," he answered. "I don't think I can promise you that

"I don't want to be there to disturb you but I won't let you take your own life either. I know you've thought about it."

Mark looked hard at her. "I don't know that I have the guts to go through with it."

"I don't think it's a question of guts. I think somewhere Nicole is still watching over you and I don't think that's what she wants. I think she wants you to carry on and be the man you can be. I think she wants you to be happy."

She didn't argue with him further. She just turned and fled to bed trying to avoid letting him see her tears. Mark knew, though, and felt like crap. He wanted to follow her but he knew where that would lead and he knew better. He made ready to go to his own bed by himself. He wanted to get an early start and solidify the plans forming in his mind. He didn't sleep much though.

211

Chapter XVIII

Mark woke up with Christine shaking his shoulder. He had turned his alarm off having finally just fallen asleep.

"Wake up sleepyhead," Christine said with some amusement. "I thought you would be up and working already."

"What time is it?" Mark yawned.

"It's quarter to seven," Christine said. "I left you to sleep for a while but then thought maybe I should wake you up so we can get to work. Are you feeling alright?"

"Almost seven," he groaned. "I'm alright, just had a lot of trouble getting to sleep."

"Nightmares again?" she asked with some concern in her voice.

"No, just had a lot on my mind and couldn't fall asleep until early this morning," he reddened avoid eye contact. "Just let me run through some stretches and we'll get to work."

Christine left Mark to himself. He got up and went through an abbreviated version of his morning routine. He looked forward to getting busy. That would get his mind focused back on the things he was supposed to be thinking about. The goal for the day was to finalize an initial plan of attack, work out when Christine would make her drops and how long Mark would stay inside.

213

Christine had breakfast on the table for him as soon as he was ready.

"Sorry I ruined last evening, Christine."

"You didn't ruin anything," she shushed. "I had a wonderful evening."

Mark looked at her puzzled. "You are way too happy right now. I do not understand."

She shrugged, "I pushed pretty hard and I expected total rejection. I thought you would either get mad at me or laugh at me. That would have hurt me deeply. Now all I have to worry about is you running away from me. Whether you'll admit it or not, we're more than just friends. That kiss last night was for me and you know it. I'll take that. I promise not going to bother you again until this is over."

He just shook his head, but she was as good as her word.

After the meal they reviewed their mode of entry and went over the plans. The toughest part would be making the hole to access the thirteenth floor ceiling space from the garbage chute. That would be their initial objective. Mark figured it would take him four or five nights to get that part of the operation completed. Once finished he would have to come out rest and revise their plans as needed. They would come back to the cottage for that. The work would then intensify. Once inside the ceiling space he could more efficient use of the time. No worries about getting a sack of trash on his head.

They spent the bulk of the next few days packaging the materials that Christine would drop for Mark to stockpile along with prepared food rations. Christine would have no trouble getting access to food but there were no grocery or convenience stores in a garbage chute or ceiling space. Mark would bring in as much as he could carry but the bottom of a garbage truck didn't offer much space for cargo.

With everything packed and ready, they left in the middle of the afternoon that Tuesday. They figured it would be easier for Christine to follow in the car while it was still daylight. They parked next to each other and then did their best to get some sleep. Mark never equipped the van to have two occupants and that didn't go so well. They would have to do something about that later because they wanted to keep the operation moving. Mark slept on the floor. Christine slept on the cot. The arrangement was not ideal because they were both a little too aware of the others proximity and that made falling to sleep difficult for both of them. Surprisingly, it was Mark who woke up refreshed in the morning not Christine, who had a bed to sleep in.

Mark rode the garbage truck in early Wednesday morning and stayed in for four days. The whole operation went like clockwork. Even Christine lost her nervousness doing her part. They remained wary though. Mark measured where to put the hole to get to the ceiling space on the other side. He bored his way through the top part of the hole first. When he got through to the other side he had missed about four inches too low. That was good news. If he had been four inches too high he would have accomplished nothing. He worked until, after four days, he had a neat rectangular hole he could crawl through. He dropped the waste material in bags down the chute. They would go out with the garbage truck and no one would know the difference.

During the day, Mark would spend most of the time in the garbage collection area because it was too dangerous in the chute, too much chance of getting hit by a sack. He would read to pass the time concealed behind some equipment. On his third day in, Cote came by on a personal inspection with an assistant. Cote took a look up the garbage chute but didn't see anything because Mark had reeled in the line. When a big sack of trash came crashing down, Cote smiled.

"Just as an added precaution Baker, I want a couple of cameras installed in here," Cote said to his partner. "We have the garbage company personnel covered but just in case I want to be able to see the garbage truck from each side when it pulls in here. How long would it take your people to install a camera on each wall and have them hooked into the main security console?"

"I can get the equipment later today and have it all installed tomorrow afternoon," the man replied.

"Good. I want you to get right on it."

With that, the pair left.

Mark waited about ten minutes before tapping out Christine's number on the cell phone. It took her a few moments to answer.

"Christine, we have a minor emergency," Mark began.

"Are you all right?" Christine asked a note of panic already in her voice.

"I'm fine. Just have a new security system to work around."

"What do you mean?"

"Don't worry yourself. We can take care of this. I'm just going to be in here for an extra two days by the look of it and I have a bunch of very specific errands for you to run."

"Let me grab a notepad and a pen then... Ok I'm ready."

"In the truck, under the box with the wiretaps, is another box that looks almost exactly the same. Inside are a couple of other pieces of equipment. I'm going to need them both but not right away. There are coils of wire and cable for hooking those up. It won't be near enough. I need you to go to a hardware store out of our local zone here and buy a hundred fifty feet of each and drop it to me this afternoon. Can we work that?"

Mark could hear Christine rummaging around in the trailer for a little bit.

"Okay, I found the case and the wires you were talking about. Kid with the Bluejays cap didn't go to school this morning so I can drop it around three thirty when the other kids come home from school. That sound good to you?"

"Perfect. I'll get back to you once all that is done. I can preinstall most of my wiring before the workers install their system tomorrow."

"What are we working on?"

"Sorry, Christine, this line is not secure so I have to cut this short. I'll tell you everything as I go or when I get back out."

"Okay, be careful."

The first part of the operation went as planned. Christine made the drop as scheduled and Mark got to work. Around six o'clock, he called Christine again.

"Great job, girl. Most of the wiring and cabling is already in place. Next comes the hard part. Getting the electronic equipment to me."

"What do I have to do?"

"I need both of those black boxes you got me wiring for and I need the laptop with the usb cable. We can't drop them because they'll get broken. We need an exact time drop off tomorrow morning sometime before eleven o'clock. Can you get in at that time?"

"Yes, the old lady with the big bag goes out at eight and usually doesn't come back before lunch."

"Good. I want you to bring those items to the twelfth floor. I plan to flatten myself against the chute wall right below my winch so the baffle from that will give me some protection in case someone decides to throw out the trash. I need you to hand the items to me directly. Understood?"

"Understood. Sounds risky though."

"No real choice. It's all part of the game we're playing. We need to do this at nine thirty sharp then. Minimizing the time I'm in harm's way is really important."

That operation went without a hitch. Mark watched Rodrigues' maintenance team install the cameras from a safe vantage point. Right after they left, he sent their system a short power surge that popped the circuit breaker. By the time they figured out that the system had overloaded and reset the breaker Mark had spliced into their new system and hooked it up to his own. He checked his systems and only had to wait for the garbage truck to visit and leave to have the needed clean footage to feed security to cover his future arrivals and departures.

By the time six days had past the solitude and tension started to get to him and he was happy to catch his ride out and get reunited with Christine. She picked him up this time with the rental car and had put plastic over the passenger seat assuming that Mark was going to be even less fresh than he was on his first trip inside the building this way.

"This has got to be the worst you've ever smelled Mark," she said rolling down the window for air and making a face. "Don't even get close to me. I'm taking you straight to the truck stop where they have showers and all. A little freshening up isn't going to be enough."

"I thought women like the smell of a hardworking man," he grinned.

"I do but you don't smell like a hardworking man. You smell like something positively rotten," she smiled back. "When we're done getting you clean we're going straight to a Laundromat and wash your clothes."

"How were things for you the last six days?" he asked, turning serious for a moment.

"It was easier because I had lots to do to keep my mind busy but it was long especially the extra two days. I'm pretty relaxed while I'm pretending to be someone else running supplies to you but waiting to see you again, and knowing where you are, is hell. I'll be so glad when this is over," she answered.

"Me too," was all he said to that.

Mark got all cleaned up as Christine prescribed and they made their way back to the cottage. They left the rental car parked in a safe place and traveled back to the cottage in the van. They both found it a long inconvenient drive but there was no real time to set up a headquarters closer by that would meet their needs. They would break for a few days packaging new supplies and reviewing the plans. Christine was now fully aware of what Mark was up to. They went over plausible stories she could feed as temporary misinformation if she got caught. They made a point of it trying not to think too much about that kind of worst-case scenario.

Now that Mark had access to the ceiling space the next step of the operation was to lay a track system. The ceiling space was too narrow to crawl around in without making lots of noise. Years ago Mark's father had designed a track system, which Mark demonstrated to Christine. There was already a practice set up in the attic of the cottage and Mark brought her up there to show her how it worked. The track itself would be attached to the top of the crawl space with adhesive. Mark would wear two harnesses: one around his chest and the other very low on his hips. A rubber wheel assembly would clip to the harnesses either the front or the back so that Mark could roll silently on the track either facing up or down with his arms and legs free to work. The system operated without a sound unless Mark got rolling fast. Most of the material Christine dropped to Mark had been track material and a good supply of it waited ready for installation.

First Mark would install a main line running most of the length of the hall with junctions at the doorway of each major room on the floor. He would then build the branch lines installing microphones and recording equipment so that they could find out what was happening in each of those rooms. Once they had gathered enough information they would plan how to strike. They needed to shut down power to the computers and backup power to them as well so that no one would be able to destroy evidence. At that point, they would render the guards, Rodrigues and anyone else who might be a threat unconscious while Marv Lindsay arrived with his buddies from the Peel police to mop up and collect all the evidence. If everything went right, that would be the end of Rodrigues and his entire organization. That would clear Mark's name and give Mark and Christine the freedom to be themselves. It looked all neat and clean on paper.

"Something bothering you, Mark?" Christine asked.

"Yes," he answered. "May sound paranoid to you but things are running too smoothly."

"How can things run too smoothly?" she asked with a bit of a nervous laugh.

"I've been doing this sort of thing for a long time," he responded. "Nothing ever runs perfectly. Usually the longer something takes to go wrong, the worse it is."

"You're really worried aren't you," she observed. "You didn't consider this new surveillance system a problem?"

"Not really. We had all the equipment to deal with it and we were in the right place at the right time to neutralize it with barely a missed step. I don't think it would bother me if it was just my life on the line..." he said, looking her straight in the eye, "but you are in just as much danger as I am."

A few days later they were back in Brampton with Mark working to build his track system and installing surveillance equipment. It progressed with tremendous speed because he could work during most of his waking hours. Christine started making her drops from the fourteenth floor and above so that Mark, with the use of a net, could catch them before they went all the way down. He didn't enjoy going down real early in the morning and sifting through the garbage to find his supplies. The surveillance Christine did on the outside allowed her to imitate a few more people in the building and sometimes she could make up to four drops in a day. It was hard work but progressed faster than Mark would have ever thought possible.

Chapter XIX

Christine had one extra mission this trip and that was to pay Marv Lindsay a visit in the evening when Mark was guessing he would be home. He had guessed right but it wasn't Marv who answered the door it was Mrs. Lindsay a short good natured round woman.

"Good evening dear," she asked. "What can I do for you?"

"I'd like to speak to Marvin Lindsay," Christine answered hoping she had the right address."

"Come on in and wait by the door dear. I'll see if he can speak to you right now. May I ask your name?"

"My name is Christine Jette and I'm carrying a message from Mark Rathman," she answered.

Mrs. Lindsay's brow went up at the sound of Mark's last name as if it meant something to her and then bustled off to fetch her husband. It took him a few moments to realize who his visitor was but when he did he invited her to come into the living room and have a seat.

"You look a whole lot better than you did last time we saw each other," he said. He came over and had a look at the thin reddish line scar covered with makeup that was the only reminder of the beating she took. "That's healed up very nicely."

"Pretty little thing, isn't she," Mrs. Lindsay added in a motherly tone.

Christine blushed. "Mark has been taking really good care of me," she said not knowing quite how to reply.

"I'm sure he has," came the response from Marv. "Just the fact that he hasn't shipped you off somewhere away from the action suggests he doesn't plan to stop any time soon."

"Are you planning on having children soon," Mrs. Lindsay asked all excited now.

By this time Christine, was crimson. This was not the conversation she had prepared for and this was out of her control now. These people were friends she could count on. They had known Mark since he was a baby but she felt more uncomfortable right now that she did during the day sneaking into a building running supplies to someone else who wasn't welcome there. Lindsay who found the situation entertaining decided it to rescue her and address the business at hand.

"If I know Mark, you aren't here to just make a social call," Lindsay said amused at Christine's discomfort. "Mark must have something big going down and you're here to bring me in on it."

Christine was relieved and launched in to her story. She told Lindsay everything that she and Mark were doing and what the plan was. Marv listened to every detail. He made no effort to interrupt until she had laid out everything. He hesitated for a period of time just thinking.

"How long do the two of you expect it to take yet before you are ready to move?" he asked after a long pause.

"Mark wants to move very carefully so he doesn't expect to be ready for another two weeks," she answered. "He doesn't want a big shoot out and he doesn't want them to have a chance to wipe any computers."

"I have a couple of old friends in the Peel force and could probably get a couple of cruisers on site at the drop of a hat. My guess is that you're going to need more than that. I'll see what I can count on and we can get back together to talk again. Can you be back here in about three days' time?" he asked.

"I will be back then," she said.

"I'm surprised Mark is letting you help him with this," Lindsay said to her.

"I don't think he wants to," she answered. "I told him that I wanted to stay and help at least for my own freedom. Since then he hasn't been able to deny that we work well together."

Lindsay nodded at that. Christine didn't want to be impolite but she really needed to go and get some rest for the night. She managed to make a graceful exit but not before Mrs. Lindsay could press a bag of cookies on her for Mark and get a whole string of advice on how to make him happy. She liked the woman but realized that her reality was not the same as everyone else's. She got a big friendly hug before she exited safely out the door.

Mark would be coming out again with the garbage truck in the morning and she looked forward to being reunited. She was hoping that in two weeks this would be all over. It still seemed like a very long time to go. Even though they had been working for longer than that on this whole operation. She curled up on the cot in the back of Mark's old van missing him as much as ever. She slept well though because she was very tired. It had been a full day.

Next morning, Mark came out safe and sound. Only difference was that he didn't smell like rotting garbage. It was obvious that he was spending most of his time working in the ceiling space. He told her that the track was all laid and almost all the microphones and recording devices were in place. They would be analyzing data as quickly as possible after that to decide how to best neutralize the place. Christine told him of the visit with the Lindsays. She jokingly told him off for not warning him about Mrs. Lindsay. He laughed when she told him about that part of the visit. He remembered what she was like and apologized for giving no warning. It had not even crossed his mind until she recounted the story to him. He sampled one of the cookies from the bag. It was almost too hard to eat. Just like he remembered them.

"Did you try one of these?" he asked her indicating the cookies.

"No," she answered.

"Good, then I have a chance to warn you about something. You might just break a tooth on one of these. They taste good but they are really hard," he advised her. "My little brother and I used to take them and smash them with a hammer or something and then eat the little pieces."

Christine laughed herself almost to tears. "I like her but she's a little strange."

They decided to stay in the greater Toronto area while they analyzed the audio information. They could gather the information more quickly and have things ready as fast as possible. They only had one last shipment of materials sitting in the cottage and that was the chloroform. They would leave that up there until everything was in place because they hadn't quite decided the best way to deploy the stuff. They would try and coordinate a date with Marv Lindsay in a couple more days.

Mark asked Christine if she spotted any kind of stake out watching the Lindsay's place. She had seen them. She had arrived on foot so there was no chance of them picking up on her license number. Mark didn't like the sound of it. If they saw her visiting more they might start checking in to it. Mark didn't want to attract any undue attention Marv Lindsay's way. He didn't need that kind of complication at this point in the game. He would have to modify the meeting and figure out a way to let Lindsay know.

There was good news though. The microphones were yielding more information than expected. The recordings Mark brought with him from right after installation already located everybody and everything on that floor. Mark would double-check his information but he had enough to start putting together a preliminary plan.

The big trick was getting a message to Marv Lindsay. They decided to write him a message to go out to dinner with his wife and meet Christine along the way. Christine would drop the note in their mail box while Mark pretending to be a delivery man with a parcel parked his van in the middle of the street to block the view of the stake out car so they wouldn't see Christine make the delivery. They pulled it off without a hitch. They then rented a motel room where the Lindsay's would pick up Christine who would be a niece visiting from out of town. They would exchange information over dinner and Christine would pass a prepaid cellphone to Lindsay so he could communicate directly with Mark without detection over the next couple of weeks.

Mark was back inside when the meeting was made. He was working hard at tapping into communications. He had worked out very quickly which room was Rodrigues' office. It was more of an office apartment so that Rodrigues never had to leave the building. Mark tapped into that phone line first. There were two small suites at each end of the floor used for guards. They were manned twenty-four hours a day with two guards each. There were another two guards roaming the halls. They searched and disarmed everyone coming up the elevator. The rest of the floor was offices and computers.

The floor was connected to the electricity running through the rest of the building. It could be switched to its own independent system in case of a power failure. Mark also had the capability of unlocking the front door so that the police could just walk in. Mark had already set things up so that he could disable everything except for the individual emergency lights. He didn't want anyone wiping computers when he made his move. The information stored in those computers would identify everyone connected to this organization. It would bring the whole thing crashing down and also clear Mark's own name. Just another week of preparations and he would be able to neutralize the whole place without bloodshed.

Christine arrived at the motel in plenty of time to get ready for dinner with the Lindsays. It was supposed to look like a pleasant meeting of relatives over a meal. They were going to a classy place at Mark's insistence and expense because he figured it was less likely to run into undesirables. Christine wore her black dress that had so impressed Mark and waited for the Lindsays to arrive. She realized that this whole operation was coming close to the end, one way or the other. She was looking forward to living a normal life again. She hoped that normal life would include Mark, if normal with him were possible.

The Lindsays arrived right on time and Christine got into the back seat. She was ready for Mrs. Lindsay's curiosity about all things personal. Christine was forced to reveal that she and Mark were just friends working together. Mrs. Lindsay was not easily dissuaded though and managed to talk Christine into revealing that she did have strong feelings for Mark.

Dinner was pleasant. Lindsay himself was sure he could get the necessary personnel to Rodrigues' headquarters to mop up as soon as everything was ready to move. The date for the following week was agreed upon. In case of emergency, they could get a smaller group of officers on the scene on very short notice. Christine was happy that this whole episode was almost over. Lindsay was a little uneasy though. The whole complex thing had been running without trouble. That almost never happened. He was surprised that nothing had gone wrong at all yet.

"As soon as Mark comes out again. I advise you to immediately run up and get the chloroform and have it ready for use," he advised. "Even partially set up that would mean a lot less trouble if things go wrong at this point."

"That's what Mark is planning to do," replied Christine. "He actually wanted to bring them down sooner but we've just been too busy getting everything else in place. He's a little paranoid that something is going to go badly wrong somewhere"

"He's wise to think that way," Lindsay responded. "It works out that way most of the time. You always have to be ready for things to go wrong. They almost always do."

Lindsay pocketed the cellphone before they parted. He looked forward to discussing the operations with Mark tomorrow afternoon, almost like working with Sam again. He was impressed with the operation and how it was set up. Mark was good and Christine was hard not to like.

Chapter XX

Christine went back into the motel room and messed up the bed making it look like she spent the night there. She left a tip for the maid tossed the key on the nightstand and left. The rental car was parked several blocks up the road so that no possible connection between her and the motel room could be made.

She didn't head straight there, though. About a block in the other direction was a corner store and Christine needed to pick up a couple packages of batteries and wanted to pick up a snack for Mark when he got out. She walked there with purpose her heels clicking on the concrete sidewalk. She still felt elegant every time she wore this outfit and he was feeling positively bubbly after her meeting with the Lindsays. She also felt a little bit dangerous with the knives Mark had equipped her with after he found out she was practicing throwing and using them. Two throwing knives were concealed around her waist and a bigger more wickedly shaped knife was strapped to her inner thigh under her dress.

Her spirits were high in spite of Mark and Lindsay's paranoia. She was sure this would be over in a week. She just knew it. She opened the door to the corner store to the tinkling of bells. She went straight to the checkout to ask the person there where the batteries were. He pointed them out. Christine picked up two packages and then made her way to the back of the store looking for something she thought that Mark would appreciate after munching pre-packaged rations for most of the last few days.

Zap saw Christine enter the store and at first did not recognize her. He did recognize her voice, though and he moved so that he could check to make sure of her identity without her seeing him. He figured he could catch her in a foot race with those heels on but he didn't want to make a scene. Her hair was done different than before and she was wearing glasses instead of contact lenses. When she tuned to get the batteries he got a good look at her face and also a couple of small distinct birthmarks on her shoulder. He was sure. He retreated around to a different aisle until he was sure which direction she was going. Then he put back the item he came to buy and went outside to wait for her.

She had her mind on other things as she came out of the store hurrying along, her heels clicking along. Zap caught up with her grabbed her arm and shoved the barrel of his gun against her ribs.

"Not a word," he commanded. "You just walk quietly along with me."

Christine recognized the voice and the smell of him immediately. Sheer terror swept through her. She wanted to scream but she was afraid he really would use the gun. There was no one on the street right close by who could help. She walked where she was directed shaking like a leaf. When they got to Zap's car he ordered her in the passenger side. With the gun trained on her, he ordered her to rummage around under the seat until she found a roll of duct tape and then ordered her to put on the seat belt. He then used the tape to bind her wrists and ankles together before forcing her to look at him so he could smile in her face. He walked around to the driver's side and got in. He didn't pull away right away. He first got out his cellphone and made a phone call.

"Cote, this is Zap," began Zapparoli. "I don't give a shit if you just went to bed. Guess what I just found... I found the girl...What do you mean what girl? The little bitch the Shadow took away from us... What do you want me to do with her... Okay I'm on it."

Zap hung up the phone and started the car. Just before pulling out on to the road he gave her another sickening grin.

"Lot of people are going to be glad to see you," he said, happy with himself. "Lucky you. Your old apartment is empty. We're only going to keep you there tonight. Tomorrow we're taking

237

you somewhere else. Don't want your boyfriend to try and rescue you too soon."

Christine tried to fight off total despair. She shook with fear but she concentrated hard and tried to get control of her fear. She blamed herself for not being careful enough. She worried that Mark might get killed trying to come to her rescue. They were so close to finishing the operation and now she felt like she ruined everything. She tried to think of what Mark had told her to say if she was caught and she couldn't think of any of it.

They drove in silence all the way to Zap's whorehouse. She was too scared to say a word and he was content to pay attention to the road and grin to himself now and then. When they arrived, Zap picked her up and slung her over his shoulder. He didn't put her down until after he had carried her all the way to her old apartment. He cut the tape and set her loose there with a warning not to do anything stupid because she would be watched. Shortly after her arrival she could hear guards posted outside her door just to be sure she wouldn't escape before morning.

As soon as he was gone Christine checked the time. She was due to make her check in call with Mark in almost thirty minutes. She couldn't do that, though, because Zap had gone through her purse and taken the phone. She sat for a long time worrying. When she had to use the bathroom.

She was careful not to let the cameras in there get a look at the knife strapped to her leg. She wanted to have some advantage over them that they didn't know about. She was grateful Zap had made no effort to search her. After a time, she managed to calm down enough to think straight and decided to try and get some sleep. Tomorrow was going to take a lot of energy.

Mark noticed the missed call right away and called her phone to see if it would pick up. It went straight to voicemail. It was possible her batteries had gone dead or she was somewhere she couldn't get a signal but deep down Mark knew something was wrong. Christine had never missed a check in call. He was worried. He had lost too much to Rodrigues and he feared losing more.

He could find a place in the ceiling space that was away from everything so that he could talk without being detected. He made his way there and called Lindsay on the cellphone. Lindsay was already in bed but wide awake as soon as he heard that Christine might be in trouble.

"We don't know for sure that she's in trouble but we can find out," Mark told him. "She was driving her car and was going to go to the van to sleep when she was done meeting with you.

Can you go and see if she got to the van? If she isn't there we know she's in trouble."

"I can do that," Lindsay answered. "Where is it parked?"

Mark gave Lindsay the location of the van and sat back and waited for him to call back. Lindsay lived a good half an hour's drive away from where the van was parked so the wait seemed to take forever. When the call finally came it was just what Mark had feared. Christine never went back to the van. That could only mean that she was picked up somewhere along the way. Mark told Lindsay to get some sleep because he might be needed on very short notice. Mark had to come up with a plan to make his hit on this place early in hopes that he could knock down everything and save Christine.

He spent a great deal of time cursing himself for letting her be part of the operation before morning came along. He tried to stop blaming himself, though, because thinking about that wasn't going to help him put together a plan. He needed to stay calm and concentrate. Hard as that was Christine depended on him and he was determined somehow to come through for her whatever the cost to himself.

First order of business was to try and even up the odds a little. There were two guards prowling the hall at all times. Mark figured he wouldn't be able to do much about those two at least in the short term. The apartments at each end of the floor. Though, were for guards and he had to find a way to lock them all in until police help could get there. It took him awhile but he came up with something. He used his equipment to bore silently through the ceiling into the door from the top. It was slow going because he could only work with the hand tools he had with him. He also had to work without making noise. The painstaking work took him most of the night. He did the steel doors for each guardroom and formed a pin out of some structural metal no one would miss right away, to hold the door shut. That would take care of the guards on each end of the hall for quite a bit of time. The other two would be a problem though. Two goons wouldn't be a problem but Mark knew these guard were trained bodyguards and would be a match for him face to face. The key would be the element of surprise. At least now he felt like he had a fighting chance.

Early in the morning he heard the phone ring in Rodrigues' apartment. Mark made his way over to that surveillance equipment. The call was over by the time he got there but it was recorded so he popped the earbud into his ear to have a listen. The caller was Cote filling Rodrigues in on Christine's capture.

"Francois, I have some great news," Cote began. "We picked up the Shadow's girlfriend. Zap's got her on ice for now."

"Good, good," he replied. "Is she hurt?"

"No, haven't laid a finger on her," Cote said. "In fact, I haven't even seen her yet."

"Good, we're going to use her for bait," Rodrigues said. "Don't forget she isn't your play thing until the Shadow is dead. Then you can do with her like you want. I'm sure that will be very special for you."

"Where do you want us to bring her?" Cote asked. "We can't keep her where she is because we know that the Shadow knows the place and I don't want him to have any advantages."

"Bring her here," Rodrigues answered. "I want to see this pretty young thing. I don't think there will be any problem with her sitting in on our meeting listening to us plan her sweetheart's demise."

"She'll be on her way within an hour," Cote agreed. "We'll have the rest of your team there at the same time. I'll have them all contacted right away."

"Get to it," finished Rodrigues. "I'm looking forward to this."

Mark was relieved to hear that no harm had come to Christine yet. Their first thought wasn't to torture any information out of her. He was thankful for that. It was also obvious that they were underestimating her. If they thought she knew what Mark was up to they would have made an effort to extract the information from her. He hoped underestimating Christine would prove to be another error in their favor.

Mark retreated to where he could make a phone call himself without being overheard.

"Lindsay," Mark said, "it's Mark. They have Christine and are bringing her here to Rodrigues' headquarters. I have a plan and a timetable. Can you get some men here at quarter to eight sharp?"

"I'll find a way," Lindsay told him. "I don't know what kind of story I'll have to cook up for it but I'll think of something."

"Great, I will call again just before you arrive with an exact time to hit," Mark told him. "I can unlock the doors and get you in the building. You'll have to climb the stairs, though, to get here. Best to go up the north stairs they'll be in the board room and you'll be closer coming for that side."

"Is Christine okay?" Lindsay asked.

"For now yes," Mark answered. "They intend to use her to bait me into the open. She's untouched at this point but she's probably terrified. Hopefully they won't clue in that she knows even a little bit of what she really does."

"Well we can be thankful she's still alright," Lindsay said trying not to sound too concerned. "What's the rest of the plan?"

"The two bodyguards in the hall will be guarding the boardroom door. The other four will be locked in their rooms until they can figure out how to break out. The only person in the boardroom allowed a weapon is Rodrigues himself. Just before I hit, the power is going out. That's why you guys have to take the stairs, besides that the elevators don't stop at the thirteenth floor without a code. I'm coming through the ceiling. I expect the guards won't be too far behind my entrance. The hard part will be neutralizing those two without getting killed myself. These two guys aren't your average goons; either one would give me a fight. I'm hoping you and the cavalry will arrive right about then and secure the place until more help arrives."

"Risky plan," Lindsay observed.

"Got anything better?" Mark answered. "I've already lost my family and a wife to these guys. One way or the other it's ending this morning."

"Good luck, Mark," Lindsay whispered.

"Thanks, I need all I can get," Mark finished.

Christine was roused awake by a pair of big, beefy, rough hands. She had fallen asleep fully dressed still wearing the outfit she wore the evening before.

"Use the toilet and make it snappy," Zap ordered.

She was surprised they let her go to the bathroom without someone with her. This way she could keep her knives a secret a little bit longer.

"What's taking so long, bitch?" Zap yelled.

"I'm brushing my teeth," Christine answered.

A key went into the door and it swung open an instant later. Zap grabbed her by the arm.

"I don't give shit what your breath smells like," Zap glared. "I just didn't want you pissing all over my car seat."

They pushed and shoved her all the way to the elevator. It was all she could do just to keep from losing her balance. Zap and one of the guards got into the front seat of his car and Christine was shoved into the back with the other guard beside her, keeping her covered with his gun. From the conversation around her, she soon understood that she was being brought to Rodrigues headquarters. That gave her some comfort. Knowing that Mark would be nearby gave her a glimmer of hope. Would he know? Would he come up with a plan? She didn't know the answer to that but she was determined not to despair. She knew that Mark would try.

When they arrived in Brampton, they drove straight into the parking garage. Cote was waiting for them. Terror gripped her again when she saw him. She remembered the beating he gave her before. He smiled at her and she felt sick inside. They herded her with them into the elevator. She tried to take a mental note of the code they entered into the elevator console but by the time the doors closed and they were moving she couldn't remember the numbers. The elevator seemed to take forever to get to the thirteenth floor. Christine held her breath as they came to a stop and the doors opened. There were two muscle bound bodyguards waiting for them. There was also an old man wiry and tough with them not a whole lot taller than her. She guessed that this must be Rodrigues. The guards with her thrust her out of the elevator so that she almost fell.

"Careful with the young lady," Rodrigues said with a trace of menace. "She may be worth more to me than any of you. Come with me, honey."

Rodrigues offered her his arm as if he were some kind of gentleman. She didn't wish to cooperate but she took the arm after a little hesitation, and he drew her a short distance away from the group by the elevator. She watched the bodyguards disarm both Cote and Zapparoli. The guards that came up the elevator were not disarmed but sent to the end of the hall where they disappeared in the apartment down there. Christine knew where they were going because she knew the whole layout of the floor. She didn't think she should show any signs that she even knew where she was. It surprised her that she had not been searched.

Rodrigues appraised her through squinted eyes. It made her very uncomfortable. "The Shadow has fine taste in women," he finally said. "Cote, had I known the real price of your services, I'm not sure I would have been willing to pay with this one. Properly trained, our friend Zap would have made a lot of money over the years with this young lady."

Cote just nodded agreement, as he was not the one in charge here.

"Christine Jette, or is it Rathman now?" Rodrigues asked, not expecting an answer. "You know, I don't have to give you back to that sick but very useful man over there."

Christine remained silent, afraid to say anything. Afraid to give away the knowledge she had, afraid to jeopardize Mark and afraid of these men who were holding her captive. Rodrigues patted the hand in the crook of his arm.

"Not to worry, my dear," he said. "I don't expect the Shadow's woman to betray him easily.

Come, you are invited to attend our little planning session where we will make a few decision concerning you and your man."

Rodrigues then led her and the rest of the group down the hall to a double door. The bodyguards took up position on either side before the group entered. Christine was surprised to see about a half a dozen men already there seated around a large boardroom table.

Chapter XXI

Mark could visualize everything going on in the floor below him.

Lindsay parked a few blocks away with three police cruisers out of sight. They would move in as soon as Mark gave the word. Lindsay had only given the officers with him a cursory briefing.

As soon as the two extra guards that accompanied Christine's entourage entered the guard apartment at the end of the hall, Mark slid his makeshift bolt into place. Then he rolled to the other end of the hall and put the other bolt in place. He then made his way back to the boardroom, where he already weakened the ceiling in advance. A good kick would cause that whole section to break free and fall flat on the boardroom table. All that remained was to choose his moment.

He could hear the men below discussing what location would be best to lure the Shadow into the open so they could kill him. When they had come to an agreement, they gave Christine back her cell phone.

"Call him and tell him you're alright and then give me the phone," he heard Rodrigues say.

"I can't," she answered.

"Why not, bitch!" came Cote's angry bark.

"Because he keeps his phone off until I'm supposed to call him. He isn't expecting me to call until noon. All we'll get is his voicemail," she answered, her voice thin and trembling with fear.

"Liar!" Cote came back.

"See for yourself," she answered in an even high-pitched voice.

Mark heard the cell phone slide across the table. He turned off his phone so that it would do as Christine said. He wanted to hug her right there. He hadn't expected her to handle things this well. This would throw off Rodrigues' timetable and when the call did go to voicemail she would know that he waited, listening, getting ready to make a move. He had to calm himself, though. He had a strong urge to crack heads. He couldn't afford to let his emotions rule. Cote made the call with the speed dial and cursed loudly as he got the voicemail box.

"Call him anyway and leave the message, but don't hang up when you've told him you're all right. Hand the phone to Rodrigues," Cote ordered.

Christine followed those instructions. Mark smiled in spite of the situation. He couldn't have asked for a better teammate. As she left the message, Mark could hear her calming herself. She knew he was near.

Rodrigues added his part of the message, "Shadow, I know you are going to get this message.

Leave your phone turned on. We are going to call you at noon, and you better follow our instructions exactly or you can expect to find your sweetheart's mutilated corpse in the mall dumpster before the week is out. I trust you'll take us seriously."

Mark turned the cell phone back on and dialled Lindsay's cell number. He tapped the microphone twice as soon as the line answered and then turned the phone back off. With a pair of insulated cutters, he chewed through the communication line between the thirteenth floor and the general security room on the first floor. He flipped a switch on a small console he had installed earlier. It released the locks on all the entrances.

Five minutes ticked away on his watch. The police should be entering the building. With night vision goggles in place, he flipped a second switch killing the power. Almost the entire building was instantly plunged into darkness. He gave the ceiling a tremendous kick and a section a little smaller than half the boardroom table fell away. Mark lost a second pulling his goggles up because there was an emergency light in the boardroom. He then released the harnesses holding him to the rail and he followed the ceiling panel. It was hard to time the landing correctly, but he managed to, hitting the tabletop with a grunt. The people seated at the table were too surprised to even move. Mark in his dark outfit with the night vision goggles on his forehead looked like something out of a nightmare in the glare of the emergency lighting. He rose to a crouch as the double doors burst open and the guards came crashing in. The first one dropped his gun as a throwing knife went all the way through his forearm between the bones.

Mark saw Christine throw at the second guard as he was bringing his gun to bear. It wasn't a great throw but it caught the guard just under the right eye and threw off his shot. The bullet grazed Marks side under his right arm and caught Cote full in the chest throwing him against the wall where he crumpled to the floor. The second guard went down with Mark's second knife in his chest. The first gun clattered to the floor not far from Christine who dived after it.

Zap was right behind her. She got to the gun but didn't have time bring it to bear. She made a vicious slash with her big knife, which a surprised Zap managed to dodge. He didn't dodge a kick from Mark though, who, like a gymnast on a pommel horse swung his body around and caught Zap full in the mouth. The big man staggered backward spitting blood. In the melee, Rodrigues took advantage of the confusion to escape into the hall through the open doors. He ran well down the hall before Mark managed to retrieve the second guard's weapon.

When Mark looked up, Christine held her knife to Zap's throat, pure venom in her eyes. "I'm going to cut your fucking head off, you bastard," she screamed.

"Whoa, Christine, back off and let the police have him. He isn't worth it. Lindsay'll be here in a minute."

She took a few deep breaths, shaking with anger, before backing off. Mark handed Christine the gun he had retrieved and then herded the gangsters to the back of the room so it would be easier for Christine to cover them. He also retrieved the knives. He gave Christine's knife a kiss before he gave it back to her.

"No funny stuff, understood," Mark growled at the men huddled at the back of the room. "Trust me, she will not hesitate to shoot any of you if you look like you're going to make trouble. Zap, you sit there real quiet. She might just shoot you for the hell of it." That's when Lindsay arrived with three more officers.

"Mark you're hit," he said with some concern.

"It's nothing, just a scratch," Mark answered. "Did you see Rodrigues?"

"Yeah he loosed off a couple shots at us. He's on his way down the south stairs," Lindsay replied.

Mark took a quick look under the table and spotted the button at Rodrigues' seat.

"Give me your radio," Mark said to Lindsay. "Rodrigues has some kind of remote device under the table. I suspect he has help on the way. Have to warn the men outside. Who's in command down there?"

"Brady," came the reply.

Lindsay handed him the radio without a second thought. Mark didn't know why he chose the words he did but he did.

"Brady. This is Sam Rathman of the Niagara Regional Police I've been on this case undercover. We need back up lots of it. We have an officer down and multiple injuries. A fugitive is coming down the south stairs. He has help on the way. I suspect they will be heavily armed. I advised you to take cover immediately."

Mark then turned to Lindsay. "Let's go get him. You take the stairs. I'll go out the way I came in and try to head him off. He's over seventy; he won't get down those stairs very fast."

Lindsay and Mark sprinted down the hall. Mark climbed into the garbage chute while Lindsay headed for the stairs. Mark slid down to the garbage below. He went as fast as he dared. There was a regular door next to the double doors for the garbage truck Mark exited the building there. As soon as he was outside he could hear gunfire up front. A burst of machine gun fire convinced him he had not overestimated the help Rodrigues had summoned.

Matthew Brady took the warning on the radio at face value and called for immediate back up. He was still on the radio when a four by four roared out of the parking garage and screech to a halt broadside to the two cruisers. One of the occupants stood and swung a windshield-mounted belt fed heavy machine gun in his general direction. Thankful that he was standing next to the car instead of sitting inside he dove behind it hoping that the engine and transmission would have sufficient mass to keep him alive. An instant later his favourite cruiser didn't have a single intact window. Bits of them were scattered all over him and the surrounding walkway. He glanced back and was relieved to see Selenski behind the second cruiser in the same position as himself. There was a scratch bleeding on his cheek but when Brady moved to help, Selenski waved him off.

The silence after that first murderous volley was worse than the gunfire. Brady signalled his partner to stay put while he crawled forward to sneak a peek around the front of the wrecked police car. A siren could now be heard in the distance. He gripped his .38 trying not to think about how outgunned he felt. When he dared poke his head around the corner, he was not surprised to see the gunner on the truck standing ready scanning for movement. A third figure in black approached them from behind. He pulled his head back and shouted to Selenski to hold his fire. He hoped his words would at least give a bit of a distraction. At the same time, he signalled his partner to get ready to move forward. Then he peeked around the corner again just in time to see the gunner landing hard on the pavement. The driver was also on the ground, trying to roll clear of the action. The man in the black outfit was not far behind.

Brady and his partner sprinted out from cover guns drawn. They weren't needed. The first man made the mistake of trying to fight. Brady winced when he heard the man's elbow break. The accompanying howl of pain was silenced with a quick knee and elbow rendering him unconscious. The second man managed to roll to his feet, knife in hand, crouched ready for action. Moving like a big cat, the black clad figure drew two knives of his own twirled them like mini batons and dared his opponent to fight.

"Drop it asshole! Or I'll let him carve you up!" shouted Brady.

He tossed the knife aside and lay face down on the pavement. Good to see he understood the drill. While Brady put the cuffs on him, he man in the black outfit moved to the door at the base the stairwell just as it opened. A creepy scrawny old man came out with a gun. He had it for less than a second and was sent sprawling on the grass. He lay staring up into the barrel of his own gun. Seconds later an out of breath Lindsay burst out of the same door.

"Don't shoot him, Mark," came Lindsay's voice. "He's done and finished. He'll spend the rest of his life behind bars."

Police cars were pulling up one after another at that point. A large group of officers made their way up the north stairs to take over the thirteenth floor and start collecting evidence. With his turkey all trussed up, Brady made his way to Mark and Lindsay.

"Are you Sam Rathman?" he asked Mark.

"This man here had Sam Rathman murdered seven years ago," Mark said pointing at Rodrigues. "I'm his son Mark."

"Your warning saved our lives down here," he said with some emotion. "Nice job taking these guys down for us. You have to be the most capable officer I've ever met."

"I'm not a police officer," Mark stated to him simply.

"Um... Mark?" Lindsay began. "You don't need to keep pointing the gun at him."

"I still want to blow his head off," Mark responded.

"Mark he's not worth it," Lindsay said.

"I want the police reports to exclude any part me and Christine played in this," Mark said keeping gun trained on Rodrigues' head. "I don't want any references as to how I got in this place."

"But Mark this could lead to a great career," Lindsay protested. "There isn't a police force in the country that wouldn't want you."

"I don't think that's the direction I want to go," replied Mark.

"But Mark you'd make a great cop," Lindsay persisted.

"I want peace and quiet for a while," Mark said. "I'm not going to get that if my part or Christine's part gets recorded in full. If I decide later to go into law enforcement, I don't need this kind of recognition to get there. You know I have the ability to make the grade if that's what I want."

Lindsay thought hard for a minute and said, "Brady are you prepared to write your report without those details and do you think we can get the rest of the boys to do the same?"

"If that's what he really wants, that's what we'll do," came the reply.

With that agreement, Mark handed Rodrigues' gun over to Lindsay. Rodrigues was taken into custody right about the same time Christine came scurrying out of the front door of the building frantically looking for Mark. He saw her before she saw him and started heading her way. When she saw him, she moved as quickly as her heels would allow. As soon as she got to him she grabbed him and hugged him hard and started crying.

"I'm so sorry I screwed things up Mark. I almost got us both killed."

"You didn't screw anything up," he answered. "Something always goes wrong. You handled yourself beautifully under pressure."

"Mark, I was so scared."

"So was I," he said holding her tighter. "I was afraid I was going to lose you."

"Mark you're hurt. I'm getting blood on my arm," she said noticing his injury.

"It's just oozing a little. I'll have the paramedics clean it up after I send you off."

"I want to stay with you."

"I cut a deal with the police here so that we can walk away like we were never here. I have to wrap up some loose ends. Retrieve my equipment and pack it in the truck. I want you to retrieve your car and bring it to the cottage. Officer Brady here will see to it that you have a ride back to your car. I plan to be home myself with the van late this afternoon. We can talk about the future this evening. Okay?"

She departed with obvious reluctance and Mark with the help of a couple of officers went to work.

Chapter XXII

The cottage door flew open and Christine had her arms wrapped around Mark, hugging him close before he got halfway across the driveway.

"Easy there, girl. I'm a little tender on the right side," Mark said wincing with pain.

"Sorry," she apologized shifting her hug to his left side. "I'm relieved to see you."

"Why? You thought I wasn't coming back?"

"I thought maybe you tricked me and headed to Montreal to pay your respects without me. You had your cell phone off all day. I worried I might never see you again."

Mark grinned, "I turned it off because the battery was almost dead and then forgot to put it on the charger on the way back here. You handled yourself well today, you know."

"Are you just saying that?"

"No. Most people would have just gone to pieces. You didn't. The cell phone business in there was nothing short of brilliant. I don't think anyone could have handled that better. Besides that, had you not thrown that knife, I wouldn't be here talking to you right now. You were a great team mate," he said squeezing her just a little more fiercely for a moment.

"How bad are you hurt?"

"Bullet ploughed through the skin on the side of my rib cage. Stung and burned like the dickens when it happened. Paramedics cleaned it up pretty good though and now it only hurts if something puts pressure on it. By the way, Cote is dead. The guy you hit in the eye with your knife is going to be fine though. Your knife missed the eyeball itself and didn't go in very deep."

"Let's get you inside and cleaned up," Christine said releasing her grip on him. She led him into the cottage where the aroma of supper hit him as soon as he went in the door.

"I'm starved. Supper smells really good."

"You aren't getting anything until you're all clean, buster."

She continued leading him all the way to the bathroom. A change of clothes lay folded on the toilet seat waiting for him.

"Now let's have a look at that wound."

"I can take care of it myself. It isn't that bad."

She smiled, "I'm your nurse now. So shut up and show me."

He shrugged and pulled his shirt up and over his head. She gasped when she pulled the dressing away.

"Not very pretty, is it? Your own fault, you demanded to see it. It'll leave a nice scar but it isn't my first." He reached up and drew his thumb across the small scar on her brow. "Now let me get washed up. I don't want to keep that supper waiting."

Christine retreated. Her mood mystified Mark a little. She seemed happy that he had not just taken off on her but at the same time he sensed stress and pain. He hoped he hadn't read her wrong as he took a small blue velvet box out of his pocket and laid it on top of his stack of clean clothes. Women could baffle him. Especially one's he really liked a lot.

He showered, being careful not to get his injury wet. He took his time making sure the rest of him was clean. He shaved and put on the comfortable clothes Christine had picked out for him. Sweat pants and sweat shirt just like she was wearing only different colours. She must be planning to stay in, lounge around and talk... when the ice melts.

Supper turned out to be a silent affair. Christine put a lot of work into the meal with the time she had. He noticed that she had somehow found a table cloth and some candle holders. Something bothered her, though, and Mark wasn't doing a good job punching through her gloom. At last she brought in a cake she had made herself and put it on the middle of the table. On one half of the cake a blue inexpertly drawn cage with its door wide open sat and all the way on the other end of the cake were two stick figures walking away. Mark knew the tall one represented him and the short one Christine. They were holding hands. At least he had one positive sign here. She served them both a piece but didn't pick up her fork to eat.

"I suppose you want to get an early start tomorrow," she almost whispered.

"Yeah," he answered not sure where this was headed. "The earlier we leave the more time we'll have when we get there. I figure we can see a couple friends before I take you home..."

"...then you'll finally be rid of me," she finished for him, a tear rolling down her cheek.

Mark sat stunned for a second, understanding sinking into his mind.

"I should have known. I'm sorry Christine. I keep thinking you can read me like a book. Grab a jacket I'm taking you for a walk on the beach. The wind off the lake is still pretty cool. The dessert will still be here when we get back. I want to show you something."

She dried her eyes got her jacket and joined him without argument. Soon they were walking on the beach away from Wasaga Beach. The sun would be setting soon but they would be on their way back before that happened. Mark wasn't planning to make this into a major trek.

"I'm going to show you something that will put your mind at ease about my intentions for tomorrow."

She looked up at him dry eyed now. "You plan to visit Nicole's grave tomorrow but you won't let me come with you. She meant an awful lot to you, didn't she?"

"She did. I'm going to talk to her there, privately. I'll probably cry some. I don't really want you to see that. When I'm done, I'll come back to the truck. I'm going to need you to hold me and hug me some then because I'm really going to feel like shit."

"I wish you felt that way about me."

"After our dinner date you kissed me and held me and told me you loved me. I think about that every time I look at you now. I didn't think I could feel that way about anyone except Nicole. I didn't even want to admit it to myself but I do feel that way about you."

A big weathered stump lay half buried in the beach at this point where Mark stopped.

"You brought me here to see a stump...?"

"No, it's something for you to sit on while I show you something else."

Christine sat down with a look of baffled curiosity written all over her face. Mark went down on one knee facing her and took her hands into his.

"I'm more nervous than I was this morning before I crashed through the ceiling. When I said I'd take you home, I hope you understand I mean our home." He fumbled the blue felt box out of his pocket and opened it, taking out a very simple engagement ring. Christine just stared in surprise. "Tomorrow I'm going to say goodbye to someone I loved with all my heart. I don't plan to say goodbye to you. Christine, I love you and I hope you don't think I'm getting ahead of myself. Will you marry me? I want to stay together."

Christine took the ring, disbelief still written all over her face. She fumbled it onto her finger and then threw her arms around Mark's neck knocking him off balance.

"Yes!" she answered as the two of them tumbled to the ground. Mark lay sprawled on his back with Christine hanging on tight around his neck next to the stump.

"Um, do you think you could let me get up? There are a lot of little sticks in the sand and I'm not very comfortable."

Christine started to giggle. "I wasn't planning to bowl you over but I kind of like where I am. If you really want to get up, I don't think you need my cooperation."

"It would be a lot simpler." He said drawing her to him so that he could plant a fierce kiss on her mouth.

She relented and they scrambled to their feet. She brushed the sticks and sand off his back before putting her arm around his waist and moulding herself to his side.

"So what are we going to do after tomorrow?" she asked

"I was hoping we could figure that out together. Before I got emotionally tangled up with you, there wasn't a day after tomorrow."

"I want to come back here for a while. Maybe we could put the Pretty Fang in the water and go sailing. I've always wanted to do something like that. The weather has gotten warm enough now that summer is here. We'll have lots of time to be together and think things through."

"We could do that."

"How long do you want to wait before we actually tie the knot?"

"Don't really want to wait."

"Neither do I but I do want at least a small ceremony with just family and a few friends. Nothing big but it'll take a little while to plan. I'm staying with you from now on though. I don't really care what anyone thinks."

"That suits me."

"You thinking about becoming a police officer like your father?"

"My specialty is undercover. You've been through the stress of my undercover work already.

Do you want to live with that off and on for the rest of your life?"

"No, definitely not."

"I didn't think so."

"I was just thinking about how much you thrive on action. Just kicking around home is going to drive you nuts. I don't want to bore you to death."

"We have lots of time to figure all that out. Tonight though we have to get some sleep if we're going to get an early start tomorrow. Montreal is a long drive and it has been a very long day."

They made their way back to the cottage exhausted but happy. By the time Christine finished in the bathroom Mark lay fast asleep in his bed. Christine peeked in and tiptoed to the bed, knelt down and rested her head on her crossed arms close to his face. She noticed the stress lines at the corners of his mouth were gone.

"Mark, are you awake?" she whispered.

He didn't respond. Just the steady rise and fall of his breathing.

She smiled, "No nightmares to wake you. No ghosts to haunt you. I won't wake you, either. I somehow doubt living with you is going to be boring for long. *Je t'aime, Mark.*"

With that, she crawled under the covers and snuggled next to him and soon fell asleep herself.

Fin

About the Author

Pico grew up in Fenwick, Ontario, Canada, a small village west of Niagara Falls. Four years earning a Bachelor of Arts in Southern California were only the beginning of his travels. He has lived at numerous addresses across Ontario, Quebec and New Brunswick. Currently he, his French-Canadian sweetheart and their five children call Moncton, New Brunswick home.

Writing is just part of his life. He still works full time in a call centre and has ambitions of operating a small woodturning business once he managed to find accommodations where a woodshop would not be an issue. In his youth he was involved in sports and played basketball and volleyball. He is still an avid cyclist using his bike to commute daily to work.

He does have a writing blog called "From Pico's Pen" and is delighted to have visitors interested in the inside scoop on his writing. Web address is http://picosplace-pico.blogspot.ca/

Thank you for reading *Let Sleeping Dogs Lie*. If you have questions or constructive criticism you can contact the author at Pico@inknbeans.com.

Look for these other fine authors from Inknbeans Press:

Annarita Guarnieri, *The Importance of Being Shine*
Emjae Edwards, *You'll Wake Up One Morning*
Susan Wells Bennett, *The Brass Monkey Series*
Jim Burkett, *The Nick West Series*
Rusty Coats, *Out of Touch*
Kitty Sutton, *Mysteries From the Trail of Tears*
Dawn Hood, *God's Pinky Promises*
David Rowinski, *The Open Pillow*
Dorothy Legge, *Poems of Faith and Love*
Ey Wade, *In My Sister's World*
Perle Butcher Lyon, *The Dutch Doctor*
Eric Pullin, *Digweed the Cat*
Hugh Ashton, *The Deed Box of John H Watson, MD*
Nickie Storey, *The Grimsley Hollow Series*
Jt Sather, *How to Survive When the Bottom Drops Out*
Virginia Czaja, *Get Real*
Jackie Williams, *the Tori-Jean, No! series*
Liam McCaughey, *Collected Werks*
Kristann Monaghan, *The Running Experiment*

Fresh Books Brewed Daily